I0545168

COLD KILL

Windtree
Press

COLD KILL

Pamela Cowan

Windtree
Press

Copyright © 2017 Pamela Cowan

All rights reserved.

ISBN-13: 9781944973391 (pbk.)

ISBN-13: 9781944973407 (ebook)

Windtree
Press

818 SW 3rd Avenue, #221-2218
Portland, OR 97204-2405
855-649-0821

10 9 8 7 6 5 4 3 2 1
Printed in the United States of America

DEDICATION
To my fellow volunteers at Emergency Operations
It was a great 12 years and you were the best crew, ever.

ACKNOWLEDGMENT

Thank you to my readers and editors: Jason Bainbridge,
Jeanne Bainbridge, Jim Cowan, Tracy Fox,
James McCracken, Tim Rautio, Sonya Rees and
Rose St. Martin Reith.
What would I do without you?
Not very much.

Special thanks to those professionals who were kind
enough to spare their time and expertise. These include,
Christina Stephens, Youtube's "Amputee OT," public
speaker, peer educator and occupational therapist, for
her invaluable insight into the daily life of an amputee.
Officer Scott Hanley, Hillsboro, OR Police Department and
Officer Scott Plantinga, San Francisco, CA Police
Department for sharing their knowledge of police
department procedures.

Any creative license taken, or errors made, are mine.

CHAPTER ONE

Monday, June 27, noon

She was a small girl but she put up a hell of a fight. Chuck gave her credit for that. He'd had to hit her twice with the blackjack—the leather-clad club he preferred—to get her to stop kicking at him.

His recruit division commander at Great Lakes, the Navy's boot camp, would have called her gutsy and that wasn't a term the old bastard used often. Chuck had busted his ass trying to impress the man, but he'd never been called gutsy.

Well that had been a long time ago. No use replaying old Navy shit. There was enough new shit to deal with.

Though that was true, the many habits Chuck had acquired in the Navy were still with him. He kept his once blond, now mostly gray, hair cut high and tight. He kept his shirts and slacks starched and ironed. He walked with his shoulders back, his head up, his spine straight and despite recently hitting the big six five, he worked hard to stay fit.

He ran three to five miles each morning and followed up each run with twenty minutes of old-fashioned calisthenics. These habits served him well. Some of the women he'd had to deal with could be a handful.

This one sure had been, but not anymore. She was lying at his feet, her limbs twitching uncontrollably, her lips opening and closing while she made a funny thin sound. She reminded him of a fish out of water, flopping around like that. He hoped he hadn't brain damaged her. He'd tried to be careful, tapped her lightly right on that sweet spot above the ear, but you never knew, the brain was a funny thing.

He bent over and pulled off her shoes. Good, no more kicking. He reached into the van and grabbed the five-gallon paint bucket. It was heavy, but he lifted it out without straining. He pried off the lid. The bucket held nothing but tap water. He lifted it high, then tipped the contents over the girl, drenching her clothes and sending the smell of wet dust to his nostrils.

He nodded. The buckets had been a good idea. Anyone nosing around the van would think they held paint. That would make more sense than a bunch of jugs of water. Making sense was important. Blending in, nothing out of the ordinary, that was the key. He was an angry man sure, but also a smart man.

He'd pulled the van as close to the truck as he could, but he still had to get her into it. He rolled her onto her stomach then grabbed the waistband of her skirt. He lifted her as far as he could, but her arms and legs bumped across the ground as he dragged her awkwardly toward the truck. He had to lower her back down to get his keys out. He undid the padlock, and a fog of chilled air enveloped him as the door swung open. He gasped, sucking the mist into his lungs. It was good, like a taste of clean winter snow. It had been a warm day and a long drive. He stood for a moment, enjoying the cool, moist air. Then the girl stirred.

He reached down, pulled her to her feet, then half lifted and half-pushed her into the refrigerated space. Contact with the cold metal floor roused her. She crawled away from him, but that was fine. In her confused state, she was moving farther into the trailer, just where he wanted her to go. Her wet clothes left a trail of moisture. He watched as almost immediately frost formed along the edges. He slammed the door, shutting her in, then pulled down the latch, inserted the padlock and snapped it in place. Sighing, he rubbed his aching hands. It was good to be done.

He took a moment to catch his breath. She was small, but he wasn't that young anymore; lifting her into the truck had taken more out of him than he'd expected. He should have got one with a ramp. Getting old sucked, but there were ways to make things easier.

There was no sound at first except the humming of the backup motor and the fan that kept the refrigeration unit cold when the truck wasn't running. Then he heard a thumping sound. She must have recovered enough to realize where she was and to feel the cold. She was banging on the walls of the trailer, hammering her fists against the steel panels. Chuck walked a few steps into the woods. The noise faded quickly. He felt more confident than ever that this was going to work.

"You aren't being too confident, are you?"

Chuck whirled around and then grinned sheepishly.

Bev had been dead more than a year, and he still kept expecting to see her. She was with him of course. Just as she'd promised she would be. He could hear her, even see her sometimes. He just couldn't touch her. Death imposed limits, even on her unending love. It was hard, but he took consolation in her sweet voice, the concern she always expressed.

He answered her, "No honey, not too confident. I put a note under the wipers so if anyone sees the truck they'll read that the truck broke down, but the driver got a ride into town and will be back with help soon. No need for them to hang around after that."

"*And what will they make of the noise?*"

Chuck turned back toward the truck, where the pounding had grown in pace and volume.

"Oh that? That won't last much longer. I did the calculations. With her clothes soaking wet and no shoes on it should go quick. Just a few more hours and it will get very quiet."

"*Well that's okay then. I shouldn't have doubted you.*"

"No, you should not," he said a little too sternly. Then he softened his tone. "But I understand, and you're right, I should be more cautious. I'd better go. No reason for me to be out here. Someone sees me, they might ask questions."

"I think that's wise."

Chuck nodded and headed back toward the van. The frantic pounding from the truck had slowed. He could even catch a hint of bird song as a flock of chickadees twirled through the tree tops, flashing the white feathers beneath their wings. He bent and picked up her shoes. He'd have to get rid of them somewhere. Throw them into the next creek or river he came too. He opened the van's front door and tossed the shoes onto the passenger seat.

It was a really nice spot he decided, as he leaned back against the van. He wouldn't mind spending some time out here, maybe come back to do some hiking. He loved the smell when his boots crushed the thick carpet of pine needles and dust. Loved the way the pines and firs creaked as the softest breeze touched their highest branches. And that sky. Had he ever seen a bluer—

"Chuck?"

Chuck smiled, "I hear you, sweetheart."

"I don't mean to nag, but don't you have a lot to do?"

"I certainly do, and you're not nagging—you're right.

I should get moving. I have two more targets to deal with before I can even think about resting."

With no further hesitation, he climbed into the driver's seat, started the van and drove away, a swirl of red dust curling away behind him.

CHAPTER TWO

Monday, June 27, Morning

In early morning, the forest smelled of damp earth, rotting leaves and just a hint of blackberries. Dappled sunlight made the distant river sparkle. She could almost make out the murmur—

Somewhere a door slammed and Kayla's daydream ended, taking her from a pleasant stroll through a vast and barely explored wilderness, to her office, much less vast and far too familiar.

With a sigh, directed as much at her own perceived lack of work ethic as it was the end of her daydream, Kayla stared down at her appointment calendar. According to the pages laying open on her desk, she was scheduled to meet with eighteen different clients in the next few minutes.

The overscheduling didn't worry her. She'd be surprised if more than one or two of them showed. A wry smile lifted the corners of her mouth as she recalled her first week as a case manager in the Eulalona County Probation Department. She'd carefully scheduled fifteen minutes for each client. That first calendar, and the fact that she'd expected her clients to show up, had been an embarrassing testament to her lack of experience.

A little more than a year later, and now a full-fledged probation officer, she no longer expected much of anything but a paycheck. The job had seemed like such a great idea at first. Better than staying with the Sheriff's Office stuck in a desk job while her friends were out there doing the real job. She'd been a good cop, serious about the "protect and serve" slogan on the side of her patrol car.

She wasn't sure how good she was as a probation officer. Already she'd begun to think of and refer to her clients as offenders, a label that was almost too easy to use. Worse, she was beginning to see potential offenders everywhere. Every person she met harbored a dark secret. The man sitting in the car across from the elementary school wasn't a father waiting to pick up his kid; he was a pedophile stalking his next victim. The man whose wife was dropping him off at work no doubt had his license taken because of a DUI. The boys on the corner playing kick ball were just killing time while awaiting a drug drop.

Kayla picked up her pen and tapped it on the calendar. *All you have to do is make it to Friday*, she told herself. Just then Diane, a coworker, stepped into the open doorway.

"You busy?" she asked.

"Not this minute. What's up?"

"Nothing. Just can't look at another file and thought I'd hunt up a fellow sufferer."

"Then you've found the right place." Kayla's office was windowless, the back wall lined with gray metal file cabinets. The rest of the room held a gray metal desk, and two uncomfortable looking guest chairs, also gray, also metal.

It wasn't a cheerful theme and it wasn't the best office in the place, but it was a tremendous improvement over the dusty cubicle she'd worked in as a case manager. Besides, the ergonomically designed black leather chair left by her predecessor was a real score. Kayla gestured toward the two thinly upholstered chairs facing her desk.

Sinking into the chair nearest the door her visitor said, "See you've managed to keep it alive." She raised her chin, pointing it at the house plant that sprawled across the top of the file cabinets. The plant, and a poster of a heavily forested part of the Pacific Crest Trail, were the only decorative touches.

"Don't know why," Kayla admitted. "It doesn't get any light, I've never transplanted it and I forget to water it all the time."

"I know. That's why I come in and water it on Fridays."

Kayla bit back her initial response. *I don't need your help.* Instead she managed a more appropriately appreciative, "You do? That's nice. Thanks."

"No problem. So, what's on your agenda?"

"The usual. I've got some appointments set up and then court this afternoon."

"Anything planned for the weekend?"

"I was just thinking about that. How bad is it to be thinking about the weekend when it's only Monday?"

Diane shrugged. The question was rhetorical.

"Anyway," Kayla continued, "I'm going up to Hermits

Peak Saturday, to do snow rescue training with search and rescue. What about you?"

"Well I'm certainly not going to spend my weekend slogging around in the snow, that's for sure. We get enough winter without having to go out looking for it. I think I'll just do some search and rescue at the mall. There's bound to be a sweater that needs saving."

Kayla laughed. Diane was known for her beautifully matched outfits, carefully highlighted hair and trim figure. The PO's teased her, accusing her of trying to look like a lawyer. Since her recent announcement that she was marrying one of the richest and most powerful lawyers in the state, and almost certainly a senator in the making, most of the teasing had stopped.

"You're awful, but I hope you enjoy your sweater," Kayla told her. "I'd rather deal with the cold than the crowds at the mall any day."

As Diane started to reply, the phone rang. Kayla picked it up, said, "Thank you," and then hung up.

"Client?" Diane asked.

"Yep. That was the front desk. Guess I'd better go get him. Talk to you later?"

"Sure. Maybe we can do lunch later this week."

"Sounds good."

Kayla followed Diane out of the office, but when Diane turned left into her office, Kayla kept going down the full length of the corridor, with its industrial off-pink carpet, beige walls and abstract art.

Kayla was five foot six inches tall, with a natural athlete's firm body. She had dark brown hair cut in a long pageboy that went up into a ponytail the moment she was done working. Her dark brown eyes were wide and thick lashed. Her nose was too long, her upper lip too thin, and her ears too big. Or at least she thought so. She tended to wear cheap t-shirts with long sleeves pushed up on her forearms, tucked into no-name, dark blue, boot cut jeans and the most expensive hiking boots she could afford.

She paused a moment to smooth the front of the blazer she pulled on when she met with clients—her professional look—then opened the door to the waiting room. As always, the smell hit her first, a blend of stale tobacco, unwashed bodies and the cat urine stink of methamphetamine. She looked for her client, spotting him quickly among the smattering of other unhappy faces.

"Mr. Raye," she called out. He got to his feet in a series of jerky movements, a middle-aged man with thinning hair, a pot belly and long thin arms and legs. She called him Mr. Raye, or Jeff, but she thought of him by his nickname, Spider. The name matched both the shape of his body and the red-eyed spider tattooed on his neck. He preceded her down the hall to her office and took the seat Diane had just vacated.

Kayla moved past him, sat down and reached for his file, which sat precariously on top of a pile of identical files stacked in her in-box.

"How have you been, Jeff?" she asked.

He shrugged.

She looked at the spreadsheet she'd attached to the inside cover of the file. On it was a list of sanctions ordered by the court as part of his probation. A few of the entries had check marks next to them. Several did not.

"You still haven't attended your victim's panel, and you've only done eight hours of community service. Your probation's up in December and I don't know how you're going to get done in time."

"What do you mean get done? My probation's over, it's over."

"No, it's not," Kayla carefully explained. They'd had this conversation before, but Jeff did not seem able, or willing, to take it in. Your probation is over when you've done everything the court ordered. You signed the agreement. Remember?"

"My probation is done in six months," he stubbornly insisted.

Kayla shook her head. "I'm not going to argue with you. If you haven't completed your community service, all 109 hours," she said after glancing down at the sheet. "And if you haven't attended your victim's panel, we'll have to extend your probation another six months."

Jeff crossed his arms and legs, "accidentally" kicking the front of Kayla's desk.

She didn't react, except to lock eyes with him for a moment, then she glanced back down at his file. "Let's talk about your fines."

"Let's not!" he said leaning forward and slapping his hands on top of her desk. Through clenched teeth he growled, "If you fucks didn't have me doing all these damn classes, I'd have enough time to find a job and pay my fines!"

"That would make sense if you'd been attending

those classes," Kayla replied, knowing full well that logic was not going to work, and kicking herself for not noticing how dilated his eyes were before bringing him into her office. Thankfully the door was open, and help nearby.

Jeff leaned forward, his weight on his hands as he started to stand. His face was flushed and his eyes were locked on hers. Kayla barked at him, "Take your hands off my desk and sit down."

He started to lower himself into the chair, and for a moment Kayla thought it was going to work, that she was regaining control of the situation. Then Jeff's poorly suppressed anger exploded. He leaped to his feet, knocking over his chair. The sound of it smacking the thinly-carpeted floor seemed to fuel his anger. He lifted his hands, then slapped them on her desk again. "What makes you think you can tell me what to do? I wouldn't be here if the judge didn't make you my babysitter."

Kayla stood. Not for the first time she realized that her office was arranged in a way that forced her to pass a client to exit. She didn't have long to consider the poor planning before her attention was drawn back to Jeff. First, he used his right arm to sweep her inbox and all the files stacked in and around it off of her desk. Then he used his left arm to sweep her computer monitor to the floor. All that was left on her desk was her keyboard. He grabbed it and threw it to the ground where it burst apart with a clatter of broken keys.

Kayla edged toward the door, wishing she hadn't left her pepper spray in her purse, wishing she was carrying her gun, wishing she hadn't come to work because—with nothing left to smash—all of Jeff's attention was now on her.

As she was frantically running through possible ways to subdue him, two of her coworkers, Roberto and Scott, charged into the room and slammed him to the ground. Kayla backed up, watching as they wrestled with Jeff, eventually pinning him. Even then he screamed and thrashed, slamming his forehead against the ground. She watched Scott struggle to hold Jeff still with his arms behind his back. Roberto grabbed a handful of Jeff's greasy hair and pulled his head back to keep him from pounding his face against the floor. Abruptly the screaming stopped.

For a moment time seemed to stall. Nothing moved but dust motes, and the only sound was Jeff's labored breathing. Then the room filled with motion and noise as every probation officer, case manager and assistant near enough to have heard, responded to the commotion.

As more and more people came into her office, Kayla was shoved farther back until she was forced against the file cabinets, the drawer pulls digging into her back. Then, through the chaos, she recognized Don calmly pushing his way in, the crowd parting to let him. Seeing him was a relief. Don was a friend, but more important, he was a deputy sheriff. Probation officers were officers of the court and were required to go through the same training. Nevertheless, there was something about the gray and black uniform that gave Don an air of authority Kayla and the others didn't possess.

The two men who had been holding Jeff continued to do so while Don cuffed him. As soon as he felt the cuffs close around his wrists he whined, "Let go. Get them off me."

Don nodded and the two men got slowly to their feet bringing Jeff up with them. He stood quietly enough and Don turned to Kayla and asked, "Are you all right?"

Kayla nodded, "I think so. Yes."

"What about me? I'm not all right. I didn't do nothin'.

I didn't even touch her." Jeff's complaints fell on deaf ears. Two police officers, summoned from the city's substation in the basement, appeared in the doorway.

"I want a lawyer. Somebody kicked me. My ribs is all busted up. Somebody kicked me in the ribs."

"You're lucky someone didn't kick you in the head. Get him out of here." Don barked. "I'll meet you down there."

The two officers took Jeff's arms and lifted him from the floor, then strong-armed him rapidly from the room, down the hall and into the elevator. Kayla knew he would be escorted to a car and from there driven to the jail just a few blocks away.

"He'll be charged with attempted assault, but they'll kick him loose in a day or two," Don explained.

Kayla nodded. She was already mentally composing the narrative she'd be required to file.

"Are you really okay?" Don asked again.

"You gonna be okay?" someone else echoed.

Kayla realized that the room was full of concerned and adrenalized coworkers all staring at her, all waiting to see how she was going to deal with this. They crowded around, asking questions, offering support.

"I'm fine. Really."

"Your hands are shaking," Don pointed out.

Kayla shoved her hands into the pockets of her blazer. She didn't like being thought of as helpless or fearful, and though she appreciated Don's concern, she certainly didn't like him pointing out what looked like a weakness. Diane came to her rescue.

"Why don't you go clean up? Get a soda or something. We'll deal with this mess."

More grateful than she could express, Kayla fled. Going past the elevator she took the stairs the three floors to the basement where the least frequented of the restrooms was found. She wanted to be alone, and counted herself lucky to find the room empty. After splashing her face with cold water she dried it with rough paper towels from the dispenser. She didn't like what she saw in the mirror. Her skin was too pale, eyes open too wide and her lower lip kept trembling. It was a face made ugly by fear and she knew it too well.

Let go. She told herself. Sure, you lost control of the situation for a minute; but no one got hurt. *Breathe. Let go.* But her self-talk was falling on deaf ears. Nothing was coming through except, of course, pain; a burning, throbbing pain in her left ankle that said she must have twisted it somehow. But she knew that wasn't true.

She looked down at her left foot. It looked so normal, but of course it wasn't. Inside the beautiful Ahnu Montaras hiking shoe was a carbon fiber foot attached to a socket. Inside the socket her leg—what was left of it—was cushioned by a liner and two sets of socks. It was comfortable enough. She'd learned to accept the pressure that squeezed her left leg from just below the knee to mid-calf each time she put weight on it. What she couldn't get used to was the phantom pain that came at night or when she was stressed. Right now her ankle felt as if someone were holding a blow torch to it. She could even imagine it swelling, pressing against her shoe. Strangest of all, the pain was coming from several inches to the left of her artificial foot. Her phantom foot wasn't even content to remain inside her shoe where it belonged. It would be funny, if it weren't so damn pathetic.

Pressing the palms of her hands against her eyelids, Kayla let the memories in.

She and Tim Manning had been sent to check a report of strange lights in what should have been an empty, long-abandoned factory. When they got to the address they parked a block away and walked up. Only on television did cops pull right up to a suspicious location, putting themselves in an unknown and possibly dangerous position. She and Tim saw nothing out of the ordinary as they approached.

"Should we go in?" Tim asked.

She'd nodded, felt that little buzz of adrenaline. They'd used the lock box code provided by the property's owner, retrieved the key and let themselves in. It was a rather anti-climactic entrance, but the dark echoing rooms had brought the creep factor back nicely.

They'd cleared the downstairs as quickly as possible. Both suspected that if anyone was hiding in there they'd be upstairs. They went to the foot of the stairs and Tim had yelled, "Police! You are trespassing on private property. Show yourself!"

Nothing happened. No one responded. Kayla hadn't expected that anyone would. Keeping her eyes on the rectangle of darkness that waited at the top of the landing, Kayla eased her way up the stairs. She stayed close to the wall on the left side, her shoulder brushing the crumbling wallpaper. Tim took the right. Holding the flashlight in her left hand against her temple she extended the gun ahead of her. This way the light would shine on what she was looking at and would also allow her to see her gun sights.

She moved the light to the top of the stairs. The darkness there seemed to absorb all light, revealing nothing at all. Step by step, she climbed upward, biting her lower lip each time a stair tread creaked, and with a growing sense that something was off here. Something was really—

Two steps from the top of the pitch-black landing she heard a sound that froze the blood in her veins—an expression she'd never understood until that moment—the sound of someone ratcheting a shell into a shotgun.

Instinctively she spun, grabbed Tim and pulled him down with her as she threw herself down the stairs. The flashlight fell from her hand and clattered away, but she kept her grip on the gun. That she wouldn't let go of.

Tim bounced off the stairway wall and into her. She heard him yell but couldn't understand. There was a deafening blast. The shotgun.

Tightly packed shot, delivered from such a short distance, felt like a giant hand had grabbed her foot and shoved, hard. She slid down the stairs face first, arms out, scrabbling for a hold. There were more sharp bangs as Tim fired up the stairs, and then, silence.

She lay at the base of the stairs, gun wavering but more or less trained on the landing. Tim got to his knees beside her. "I think I got him," he said.

Then everything went very gray.

When she could focus again, Tim was standing over her, his horrified expression sent the first jolts of terror through her. She didn't want to know what he knew, didn't want to see what he saw, but she couldn't help herself.

She twisted onto her side and looked down the length of her body, or rather, up, since her head and torso were on the weathered wood floor at the foot of the stairs but her legs were on them.

Craning her neck she managed to see her feet, one still clad in a polished black shoe, the other a mass of mangled tissue and shattered bone, unrecognizable but for her pinkie toe and its neighbor, both painted, in a rare nod to female fashion dictates, Luscious Lime.

Looking beyond her toes she realized what was left of her foot was attached to her leg by a thin strip of exposed tendon. For the first time in her life she fainted.

Standing in front of the bathroom sink, her eyes still closed, Kayla used a trick she'd learned in the therapy the department had forced on her after the shooting. She let go of the memory of being shot, brought herself back to today's fresh trauma and tried to imagine the most horrific of outcomes.

What if Spider had put his bony hands around her neck, slammed her into the desk, and tossed her so hard against the wall that she bounced back? What if he did it again and again until she looked like a tennis ball being played against a backboard? She saw her arms and legs flailing as she spun, her mouth open wide in surprise.

Each imagined moment became more and more ludicrous. She pictured herself as that sticky stuff kids like to toss at walls, so that when Spider tossed her up at the ceiling she stuck. The image broke fear's hold on her and she smiled at her strange imaginings.

Rolling her shoulders to relieve the tension in them she congratulated herself on the progress she'd made. The anxiety attack was stopped before it had a chance to become full blown.

Now if she could just keep pretending everything was okay.

Returning to her office she found a cluster of her coworkers still there talking excitedly, both debriefing and calming down after the event. Thoughtfully, they'd picked up everything that had landed on the floor and placed it back on her desk. Even the keyboard and the handful of loose keys were neatly piled there. She thanked them and then shooed everyone, except for Don, back to their own offices.

"Better?" he asked, once they were alone.

She nodded, though there was still a knot of tension in her stomach and the beginning of a headache at the base of her skull, after effects of the surge of adrenaline. She looked at the wreckage on her desk in disgust.

"I can't believe how fast that happened. I've never had a client go off on me like that. He was stoned on something."

"Scared you." It was a statement not a question.

"Hell yes. Hey, do me a favor. Don't make a big deal about this if you see Stenn. No need for him to worry." Stenn was her boyfriend and Don was his friend.

"I won't tell him, but you sure you don't want to talk

to him about it? You know, just get it out."

"Oh, I'll tell him. I just don't want the story to get blown up bigger than it was. Spider's fairly harmless, a low risk offender. I was probably more freaked out than I had to be. It was unexpected, that's all. Nothing really happened. Like he said, he never touched me."

"Because someone showed up in time."

"We don't know that."

"You do know it. That's why you were shaking."

"Maybe," she admitted reluctantly. "I should have seen it coming. I've had the weirdest feeling lately. You ever felt like someone was following you, but when you look around no one's there? I'm thinking maybe I wasn't imagining it. It was probably him, getting up the nerve to give me a bad time."

"Why didn't you—?"

"Yeah, I know," Kayla said, holding up her hands to ward off both his expressions of concern and his lectures. "I probably should have told somebody, but it was just a feeling and I didn't have any proof. Like I said, I didn't actually see anyone. Spider was probably just keeping an eye on me and pumping himself up to confront me. I'm guessing he took something to amp himself up right before our meeting. Just lucky he was messed up and stupid enough to try it in the office."

"Damn, I never thought about how this could have been premeditated. I just figured you pissed him off."

"Oh, I pissed him off all right, but I'm pretty sure that's what he wanted: a reason to jump me. We don't work with the nicest people." Kayla stared blankly past Don to the poster on her wall. The call of the forest was compelling, the sound of wind in the tops of the trees, the hot sun, dust puffing up under her hiking boots, the smell of pine and best of all, being alone.

"Hey have you heard I was thinking of signing up for NMR?" Don asked, interrupting her reverie and blatantly changing the subject.

NMR was the acronym for Northwest Mountain Rescue, a state and grant funded search and rescue operation, based in Portland, Oregon, that provided volunteers to law enforcement all over the state, including the Eulalona County Sheriff's Department. Kayla, a trainee for two years, had taken nearly a year off to recover from her "accident." For the past two months, she'd been trying to make up for lost time by participating in every exercise and training she could manage. After proving she could handle the roughest trails, she'd been judged fully deployable and was looking forward to her first mission.

"Stenn said something about it," she replied, pushing a strand of hair out of her eyes and reaching for the bent wire basket that had been her in-box. "It's a long way to travel, but they have the best trainers."

"Yeah, I told Stenn we should both join, but he said he was too lazy."

Kayla made a snorting sound. "Yeah, I guess that five mile run every morning, not to mention the weight training and the kick boxing is just to fake us out. Of course, I bet your wife could take him," she joked.

Don's wife Barbara was one of the trainers at the gym where both she and Stenn worked out. Her reputation for being tough was becoming legendary.

Don shrugged, "Could be. Well guess I better get to it." He spun on his heel and was gone.

Kayla, confused by his sudden change in mood and abrupt departure, wondered if she'd said something wrong.

Sighing, she sat down and began to reorganize the contents of the folders that had slid free after being knocked to the floor. There was no point in trying to make sense of this day, but at least things couldn't get worse. As soon as the thought crossed her mind Kayla superstitiously rapped her knuckles on her desk.

CHAPTER THREE

Monday, June 27, Noon

Bobby was in a great mood. He'd just found out he was being rotated off the late shift. That meant he'd get to see Julie more than just in passing. They'd been married over a year, and he supposed the honeymoon should be over, but it didn't feel like it. Maybe that was partly because they saw so little of each other.

This had been Julie's first year of teaching since getting her degree. If she wasn't at school, she was at home studying or developing activities for her boisterous group of kindergartners. Bobby had been amazed at how quickly Julie had memorized all twenty five of their names. Of course, she was so excited and happy to finally be teaching that he'd bet she'd always remember the names of the kids in this special first class. Yeah, teaching was definitely Julie's thing, and he was fairly sure being a cop was his.

Not that he looked like one. He always thought he looked more like a young Santa Claus than anything else. Maybe he should be in a shop making toys. Thanks to his German mom, he had a round face that he thought was a little too soft around the jawline, plump cheeks that tended to flush dark pink when he was nervous—or hot—or cold. Worse, his eyes were bright blue, and did they twinkle? Of course they did.

He smiled at his own funny version of vanity, then brushed his hand across the top of his head. The new short haircut felt like the bristles of a brush. He thought the more military cut made him look a little tougher, a look more in keeping with the uniform. No one expected a cop with blond curls, yet another unfortunate genetic gift. He hoped Julie would like it. He'd had it done on his lunch break and she hadn't seen it yet.

Bobby shifted his hands on the wheel. What was he worried about? Unless she was really pissed off at him, Julie never seemed to care how he looked. No matter how dirty or unshaven he was, she always greeted him the same way. Her big green eyes would go wide, a smile would dimple her cheeks, and then a full on grin would appear. Finally, she would shriek his name and run toward him, jumping at the last moment so that her arms were locked around his neck, her feet dangling off the ground. He grinned, remembering a time when she'd jumped so enthusiastically that she'd knocked him over backward. They'd landed in a heap, laughing like mad. Too bad it had happened right in front of the station and that as they were getting to their feet he noticed the Sheriff coming down the steps. Since then he was careful to brace himself, and she'd dialed it down a bit. Despite the moment of embarrassment, he hoped she never stopped completely.

He was disappointed when he didn't see her ancient Toyota in the driveway. The old yellow Corolla she'd driven since she was sixteen was more like a pet than a car to her, and like an old pet it was incontinent, dribbling oil wherever it went. Bobby pulled in and parked in front of the garage door, on the side farthest from the front door, and next to the wide oil stain on her side of the driveway.

He didn't bother trying to park inside the garage. Shelves filled with craft supplies, poster board, crayons, and paper plates took up what they thought of as Julie's side. His side held an unfinished wood strip canoe he hoped to have ready by mid-summer. With their varied hobbies and interests Bobby knew they'd always have lots of stuff. With the poor pay that came with their career choices, he had no expectation that they'd ever own a home big enough to contain it all, or that their cars would ever see the inside of a garage.

He'd grown up in a row house in Philadelphia in a home his mom kept so uncluttered it echoed. That he and Julie had adopted an entirely different lifestyle was not unexpected or unappreciated.

Unlocking the front door and stepping inside, the vibrant colors Julie had chosen for the walls greeted him like a happy shout. At first her choice of lime green for the kitchen, orange for the dining area and yellow for the living room had seemed too much. But once the coffee brown, suede furniture was in place and the heavy framed and matted prints hung on the walls, Bobby had been forced to admit that it worked. Once he'd realized he could trust Julie's good, albeit non-conventional taste, he'd been able to relax and let her do whatever she wanted. Not that she wouldn't anyway, he reminded himself with a crooked smile. Still, even painting one wall in their bedroom purple last weekend had been more fun and less painful than he'd expected.

He checked the fridge for a note but there was none, just the last thing she'd drawn on the magnetic white board, a note that said, "Don't set yourself on fire!" a reference to the way he cooked, with the burner on high or off.

The sink held a pile of dirty dishes but that didn't tell him much. He'd had an early meeting so he'd grabbed a bagel and coffee on the drive in. He hadn't gone into the kitchen or noticed what was in the sink before he left so he had no idea what meal, or meals they represented.

He took a caffeine free diet soda out of the fridge. There were some errands he had to run and he was disappointed. He'd hoped Julie would go with him.

Normally she'd be at work now, but Friday had been the last day of school before summer break. Thinking she'd return soon he decided to wait. At the sink, he twisted the drain stopper and started running the hot water, then he added a thin stream of dish soap. As the scent of green apples filled the air he rolled up his sleeves and started washing the dishes.

CHAPTER FOUR

Monday, June 27, Afternoon

Kayla hadn't accomplished much after Don left. When she tried to turn on her monitor a blue swirl of light had appeared, followed by a disconcerting snapping sound and then a useless black screen. She'd gone to Diane's office to borrow computer time and submit a work order for a new monitor and a keyboard. Then she spent the rest of the day organizing stacks of folders, both the ones on her desk and the ones in the cabinets that Jeff the Spider hadn't had a chance to throw around. On the way out she asked the receptionist to order a new in-box to replace the crumpled one. All in all, it had not been one of her best days.

Deciding she deserved it, on the way home she swung by the bakery. She choose a chocolate brownie filled with walnuts for herself and a lemon tart for Stenn. She'd made a pot of almost-from-scratch spaghetti sauce on Sunday, so all she had to do was boil some pasta and put together a simple green salad.

"Stenn coming over for dinner?" Mona, the baker asked with a wink.

"It's Monday, isn't it?" Kayla told her, trying not to resent the lack of privacy. It was the price you paid for living in a small town. Everyone knew way too much about your life, habits, tastes and boyfriends.

Kayla took the bag of baked goods, thanked Mona, and left the store, exchanging the smell of baking bread and powdered sugar for the smell of rain on the wind, and a whiff of diesel as a truck rolled noisily down Main Street.

A renovation two years earlier had changed the face of downtown Blue Spruce. Instead of a row of businesses with fading facades and crumbling concrete sidewalks, the buildings were now crisp with fresh paint in designer colors. The sidewalks were paved with brick and wide enough for wrought iron benches for tired shoppers. There were even rows of tall, black street lamps with hanging pots filled with brightly colored flowers. The look was more Europe than Wild West. Kayla wasn't sure she liked it.

She climbed into her dark gray Jeep, a four door with custom wheels, Mud Country tires and an impressive brush guard. Kayla thought it might seem a bit heavy on the testosterone, but she found driving a mini tank with room for passengers, that could take her almost anywhere under almost any conditions, oddly reassuring.

With a quick glance at the nearly non-existent traffic, she pulled out of the bakery's parking lot and headed for her home in a quiet suburb only five minutes away.

Stenn's mud-spattered pickup was parked in the driveway of the ranch style house she rented and shared with her rarely there roommate, Emma Jean.

All Kayla knew about her was that she came from Kentucky, was in college studying something to do with blue lasers, and worked part time flipping burgers.

About the only time she came home was to shower, wash a load of laundry, or sleep. She was smart but not boastful, attractive but not flirty. She kept her best feature, her long blond hair—which Kayla envied—hidden in a single loose braid. She never hit on Stenn, was upbeat, and paid her rent and utilities on time every month, making her that rarest of creatures, a good roommate.

Finding the front door unlocked, Kayla walked in to find Stenn in the living room scrunched down on the couch, a beer can in one hand, a remote in the other.

"You look like someone I've been married to for ten years," she couldn't help saying.

"Thanks," he said, waving the beer at her. "Should I belch and ask what's for dinner?"

"I think belching after dinner, scratching before."

"Ah. I knew I should have read that book of etiquette." He set the remote down on the couch and crossed the room to give Kayla the hello kiss she needed. Though she hadn't realized just how much she needed it until she felt his warm lips on hers and the tension she'd been carrying all day slowly dissolved.

"Rough day?" he asked, reaching up to rub her shoulders. She nodded, put her head against his chest and took a deep breath. After a moment of luxuriating in the calm she felt whenever he was close, she stood straight and said, "I'll start dinner and tell you all about it."

"What can I do?" he asked.

"Open one of those for me," she said, nodding toward the can of Rolling Rock in his hand.

In a short time they were sitting in the kitchen at her old maple table, sipping their beers and sharing their day.

Kayla told Stenn about the client who had swept her desk. "Don was great. He had Spider in cuffs so fast it was like magic."

"He's a good guy, and a good cop. I know he made you mad that time on the range."

"Well, he was fine when we were competing with our handguns because he won, but when I beat him on the rifle range I thought he was going to snap his jaw, the way he was grinding his teeth."

"Man pride. Comes with the uh—equipment."

"Well, it came in handy today."

"I should have been there," Stenn said, a note of bitterness in his voice.

"Odds are you probably wouldn't have been around. Even if you were still a cop, you'd have been out on patrol somewhere," Kayla knew, even as she said it, that logic didn't matter. Stenn wasn't really complaining about missing the action in her office. What he really missed was being with the sheriff's office. She thought it was noble that he'd quit to help his sick father, but he missed his friends, his coworkers, and mostly the work he felt he'd been called to do.

Kayla had mixed feelings about it. If he'd stayed there they might never have pursued a relationship. They'd both felt an attraction, but neither had wanted the complications of an office romance, or to be the butt of the inevitable jokes and teasing. They'd only begun seeing each other after he quit. The irony was that she'd been shot not long after and had also left.

"Going to make a pot of decaf to go with dessert. You want some?" Kayla asked.

"Sure," Stenn said, finishing the last bite on his plate.

She measured out the coffee grounds and asked, "Any idea what might be going on with Don and Barb? I made a joke about her today and he got all funny, mad or upset or something. Barb and him fighting?"

"I don't know for sure, but yeah, I think they're having some problems. Seems like she puts in a lot of hours at work. At least he mentioned that a couple times."

"Well so does he," Kayla said, immediately on the

defensive for her friend. Those ten and twelve hour shifts aren't easy on any of us."

"Yeah, I know," Stenn said. "There's a reason so many cops get divorced. Bad hours. Bad pay."

"Don't forget bad attitude," Kayla joked.

"Me? Not me. I'm well trained. Watch this." He tossed his beer can into the recycling bin on the other side of the room."

"That was an example of your training?" Kayla asked.

"It was. I didn't leave it for you to put away, did I?"

"No, but you could have got up and rinsed it."

"I'm only partly house broken."

"I realize that. So for now, I'm appreciating your good aim. As tired and cranky as I am tonight, if I'd had to put it away I might have thrown it at you."

"I sort of sensed that possibility," he said with a lopsided grin. "You need a break. You have anything planned for the weekend?"

"What do you have in mind?" Kayla asked as she poured a measured amount of water into the coffee maker and then pushed the brew button.

"Carmen told me her cousin was in town and could come over and help out with dad. I was thinking you and

I could get out of town, maybe take the camper down to Diamond Lake, do a little fishing, some hiking, mostly just get out of here."

"You mean actually spend time together?"

"Overnight," he agreed, coming up behind her, where she stood plating up their desserts. He brushed the hair away from her neck and bent to kiss that vulnerable spot that always made her go weak in the knees.

The thought of spending a whole night with Stenn filled her with conflicting emotions. On the one hand, she loved the idea of being able to snuggle up against him all night. How would it be to wake from one of her night terrors and be able to reach out and touch him? She could imagine resting her head on his broad chest, listening to the steady beat of his heart and falling back to sleep in the comfort of that sound.

They'd made love but she'd always managed to keep her leg at least partially hidden. She'd kept a sheet or comforter wrapped around it, even kept one leg of her pants on once. She knew she wasn't fooling him. She wasn't subtle. Nothing about missing part of your body was. But he'd seemed to understand and not tried to pull the sheet away or touch her there. But a whole night?

Maybe if she wore pajama pants and kept the prosthesis on, even though that was bad for her skin. But what if she flung her leg across him in her sleep and he got a good look at it, or touched it by mistake. Or worse, what if she took it off the way she was supposed to, and he saw what was left of her real leg? The prospect gave her chills. It was one thing for her to get used to what had happened to her. After all, she didn't have a choice. But to expect him to accept something so . . . so . . .   She didn't even have the words.

"Honey, are you worried about your, you know, your foot?" he asked awkwardly. "I told you it doesn't matter. I don't care. I never have."

"Hey, let's just eat dessert, okay? I need some time to think."

Stenn nodded. "You take all the time you need."

"This would be a lot easier if you were more of a jerk," she chided him.

"I'll work on that," he said. Then taking their plates, he headed to the living room where Kayla hoped they'd watch the news like a pair of old married folk, eat their dessert and wind out the day slow and easy.

As Kayla poured coffee into two mismatched mugs,

she thought about how good it was. Falling for a friend, someone she already knew, someone she had worked with and respected. It was easy and also wonderful, not just because of the sex—the amazing sex—which was so good she could actually shut off her brain and forget about her foot for minutes at a time, but also because she was sick of being alone.

Ironically, being in a relationship had changed being alone from the factual state of being by oneself, into the more emotionally charged state of being lonely. She knew his leaving right after they had sex was her fault. That she was the one who asked him to go home, even though once he did the sense of loss and abandonment was overwhelming. Knowing those feelings were illogical— even crazy—didn't change anything.

Heaven help her if she turned into one of those women who lived their life as if they were acting out some dramatic play, with them at center stage. She'd always prided herself on not being like that. Still, dramatic or not, crazy or not, it was true. After he left she was miserable. Being in that bed that no longer held the weight and warmth of his body, losing that sense of safety . . . But no, that wasn't it. It wasn't safety. She hadn't truly felt safe since that shotgun blast. It was more like having a reason to get up, to make more than toast for breakfast, to think about a future that was more than just hers. Taking the coffee, and her emotions, firmly in hand, she turned back to the table.

Stenn immediately reached for his coffee and, cradling the mug in both hands, he said, "So, about Saturday—"

"Saturday. Oh hell. I just remembered," she said with a mix of regret tinged with relief. I've got an exercise with NMR on Lost Horse Mountain. I can't see you on Saturday."

"Can't get out of it?" he asked.

She shook her head. "No, they're sending trainers down here. If we want them to keep doing that we have to prove we appreciate it." Relieved that the decision had been taken away from her, Kayla felt her mood lift.

"Were you planning to sleep on the mountain?" Stenn asked.

"No," she said, immediately regretting her stupid habit of honesty.

"Then let's forget Diamond Lake and I'll just come over Saturday night. You'll probably be all cold and wet coming back from Lost Horse, so maybe a warm, naked guy in your bed won't be a—"

Kayla moved around the table, leaned down and kissed Stenn fiercely. Whatever happened Saturday night, it was nice to be wanted right here and now, and as Stenn put the palm of his hand against the back of her head and pulled her mouth tight against his, she wanted him right back.

If it hadn't been for the always possible, if unlikely, appearance of her roommate, clothes would have hit the floor right then and there. However, because of the threat of Ellen Jean's presence, Kayla maneuvered Stenn into her room, where they practiced for Saturday with great enthusiasm.

Later that evening they settled comfortably on the couch to relax and watch TV. She snuggled against Stenn as serene and self-contained as a cat. This must be how the great courtesans felt she thought. To have won the richest or most beautiful of men and to have satisfied them while also demanding to be satisfied. It could go to your head, make you buy makeup and expensive shoes. She snorted, almost choking on her coffee. Stenn looked at her quizzically. "Just a funny thought," she said.

"Not going to share?"

"Not on your life."

Stenn smiled and took another bite of lemon tart. He didn't have much of a sweet tooth so tended not to tear through his dessert with the same enthusiasm. God, he was handsome Kayla thought, every girl's dream of a cowboy, tall with wide shoulders, square jaw, shaggy blond hair and Nordic blue eyes. She felt very girlish, sitting there in her silky pajamas. It didn't even bother her that her artificial foot was in full view. Supposedly skin colored, it had certainly not been modeled after *her* skin. The foot looked tan next to her real one, which was pale and bony in comparison. Still, she didn't feel too self-conscious. It was hard to hate yourself after such an unmistakable conquest. In fact, it was hard to do much of anything at the moment except wonder how it might feel to slide onto Stenn's lap. To feel the silkiness of her pajamas against the rough fabric of his jeans. His hands moving—

Stenn looked up and met her eyes, then watched the tell-tale blush spreading across her cheeks. Nervously she pushed a strand of dark, shoulder length hair behind her ears. Even her ears were turning red. It made him smile. He'd never met a woman who was so openly herself. There were no walls around her. She wore no mask. Instead, she was honest, direct and outspoken. Sometimes he thought that was wonderful, and sometimes he thought it made her too fragile for the work she did. He could understand why she spent so much time alone, hiking in the mountains, or out kayaking on the rivers. He thought people with their hidden agendas and easy lies must confuse and overload her. Still, and maybe selfishly, he wouldn't want her to change. He loved that he could tell when she wanted him. That she couldn't conceal a single thought and didn't really try.

Besides, despite what she thought, she was pretty. So what if she didn't have a trendy hairstyle? Her dark auburn hair was shiny and always smelled like spring flowers. So what if she didn't wear makeup? Makeup couldn't improve her healthy glowing skin, her dark brown eyes were striking enough without all that black stuff, and her lips wouldn't be nearly as kissable smeared with lipstick. Kayla's occasional apologies for not being a girly girl only made Stenn wonder what she was talking about; she was all the girl he'd ever want.

Suddenly he remembered the gift he'd picked up for her. He'd meant to give it to her when they were out at the lake but no sense waiting. "Got you something," he said and reached into his pocket. "Didn't have time to wrap it." He opened his hand and she looked down at the bracelet on his palm.

"Oh, that's awesome. How did you know I wanted one?"

"You told me you did. Actually, you said you were going to make one."

"Right, as if that would happen."

She took the bracelet from his hand and held it up to the light. Woven from black and green camouflaged paracord it wasn't unattractive and was a useful tool to keep with you, especially if you spent any time in the woods. Unwoven it would provide enough tough parachute cord to serve as fishing line, to make a fire bow or help build a shelter.

She wound the bracelet around her wrist then held it out for Stenn to close the tough black plastic clasp. Stenn watched her look at it on her wrist with the same pride of ownership some might bestow on a tennis bracelet.

"It's perfect," she said. Then, with a mischievous smile she put her hand on his knee, then pushed her nails into the fabric of his jeans and drew them up his thigh.

Stenn glanced at his watch. It was getting late but there was still time. He was about to set down his coffee and pull Kayla onto his lap when his cell phone went off. "Sorry, better take this," he told her. She nodded as he snapped the phone off his belt and said, "Lehrer." He listened a moment, said a terse, "Be right there," and hung up.

"It's Dad," he told her. "They think he may have had another heart attack. They're taking him to the hospital right now. I've gotta get over there."

"Should I go with you?"

Stenn hesitated, then, "No, too many false alarms. You should stay, get some sleep. If it's bad, I'll call."

"You promise?"

"I promise. If you don't hear from me, you can assume things are going okay."

Kayla followed Stenn to the door. He pulled her in for a quick hug, then hurried out.

Kayla locked the door, then returned to the kitchen to clean up. Stenn's poor dad. He'd had a serious heart attack about eight months ago, and a series of smaller "events" since. That was the reason Stenn had resigned from the department. He'd had to take on the responsibility of running the ranch. Stenn's mother had died when he was in his twenties. His only other living relative, a sister, lived with her missionary husband somewhere in China. Someone had to keep the ranch going because five people earned their living working there and a small portion of the income went to Stenn's sister to help keep her, her husband and their four kids afloat. Besides, Stenn was sure losing the ranch would kill his father outright, and he wasn't about to let that happen.

As Kayla did the dishes she thought about the tough old man, son of Norwegian immigrants. Dad Lehrer was a tall, slightly stoop-shouldered man with a thick mane of white hair, deep wrinkles in a sun-leathered face, and blue eyes that were an age-softened version of Stenn's. He'd never said an unkind word to her, or to anyone as far as she knew. Kayla wasn't much of a church goer but she decided it couldn't hurt to send a little prayer up for him.

CHAPTER FIVE

Monday, June 27, Evening

Praying was on Chuck's mind as well, but then he was digging a grave and the two things seemed to go together. He'd driven back to the refrigerator truck just as the sun was going behind the mountains. Its rays cast a soft pink light against the jagged silhouette of pine and fir trees. No time to appreciate the view though. Chuck drove past slowly, the van's headlights glaring off the truck's white sides. He saw no other car, no other person, and sensed that he was alone out here with the night hunting predators.

This time, instead of pulling in behind the truck, he pulled the van down a narrow offshoot of the main logging road and parked in dark shadows. Then, grabbing a shovel and some gloves from the back he walked back to the refrigerator truck, taking time now and then to pause and listen.

When he reached the truck he took a pen light out of his shirt pocket and used the narrow beam of light to find and unlock the padlock. When he opened the door a wisp of mist wreathed him, momentarily blocking his sight. Even though it was cooler outside than when he'd last opened the truck, the refrigerated space was still much colder than the night. He swiped at the air impatiently; finally the fog cleared and he was able to see. The girl he'd locked inside was sprawled with her head near the door and her back against the side of the truck. She was to his left, and conveniently, just within reach. Her skin was pasty white and white foam dotted her lips and chin and moistened the front of her shirt. Her eyes were open. They flashed, seeming to move as the light swept across them.

"Ridiculous," he told himself.

"*What was that dear?*" Bev asked.

"Nothing. Nothing at all."

"*Shouldn't you hurry it along?*"

"Now Bev, no nagging, I'm moving just as fast as I should." He knew exactly what to do next; after all he'd selected the spot just for this purpose. He leaned the shovel against the truck and pulled on his gloves. Never knew where you might leave a finger print, besides, the back of that truck was damn cold.

He took hold of the girl's wrists and tugged. At first the body resisted, the joints were locked and it seemed as if she was frozen to the metal sides like an incautious tongue to an old fashioned, metal ice cube tray. But finally, with a strong tug, she came loose and nearly flew into his arms. He let her body drop to the ground, then bent over and grabbed her ankles. Luckily the half moon was rising, and the light it shed was enough for him to get his bearings and avoid the half-buried rocks and clumps of brush as he dragged the unresisting body to the ravine that paralleled the road. Grunting with the effort, he tumbled her into the gully and went back to the truck for the shovel.

A few moments later he was standing above the girl's body. Her skirt had hiked up, revealing a pair of white lace panties and slender thighs. She had a nice body; he couldn't deny that. He didn't know why he hadn't noticed it before. He supposed his mind had been on other things. Plus she wasn't really his type. He never had much cared for blondes and her boyishly short cut was not to his taste. One of the few things he'd asked of Bev was that she let her lovely chestnut brown hair grow long. Long hair was feminine, sexy; he didn't get why more women didn't understand that. Well it was a shame.

Taking the shovel he began to loosen the soil on the side of the ravine. Dirt and rocks broke loose and sifted across the girl's body and his shoes. He was surprised by how loud the tumbling rock sounded. Maybe Bev was right. Maybe he should hurry. He worked harder, jamming the shovel into the dirt, twisting, patting the powdery soil and gritty pebbles firmly around her. By the time she was buried deep enough to satisfy him, Chuck was covered with sweat and red dust. He knew he should get moving but he'd been raised to believe in God and so he took a moment to bow his head. "The Lord is my shepherd," he intoned, reciting the 23rd Psalm just as he'd learned it in Sunday school. It seemed very fitting for the occasion.

When he was finished he said a heartfelt amen, took a final look around, then climbed out of the ravine. He walked past the refrigerated truck and went to the van, using the pen light to navigate only where the shadows were darkest. He put the shovel and gloves in the back then used his fingertips to massage the dust from his hair.

"You're a mess," said Bev, her voice taking on that lilt it did when she was teasing.

Chuck smiled. "I suppose I am." He opened one of the five gallon containers and quickly washed his face and hands.

Having made himself more presentable he walked back to the truck, shut the cargo door, and restored the padlock. Then he climbed into the cab, put the key in the ignition and gave a sigh of relief when the engine caught on the first try. He'd worried that the battery might have run down. He'd brought jumper cables. Prepare for the worst and celebrate the best was one of his favorite mottos.

As he revved the engine, Chuck did indeed feel like celebrating. There was a great deal of satisfaction in a job well done. Of course, this was just the beginning, but if the rest went as easily . . . well no reason it shouldn't.

"One down, two to go, right dear?" asked Bev.

"That's right." Two more little girls before the account was settled, balance restored, and justice served.

Chuck sat quietly, the truck vibrating beneath him as the alternator fed the battery, preparing his choice of killing field for the next round. With nothing to do, his mind drifted back to that sight of white thigh and the little slip of cotton between those legs. Damn it, what a waste, and it wasn't like Bev could complain. They weren't really married anymore.

"*Don't say that Chuck,*" Bev said, her voice catching on a sob.

"Oh honey, I'm sorry. I take it back. I didn't mean it." But Bev wouldn't be placated so easily.

Once he was sure the battery was fully charged Chuck switched off the truck. Then, after making sure it was locked up tight, he walked back to the van, looking forward to getting back to town, taking a shower and getting some shut eye. He wished Bev would stop her yammering about his dirty thoughts, but he'd driven more than halfway to town before she finally got around to forgiving him. Sometimes Chuck thought it had been easier when Bev was alive, at least then she couldn't read his goddamn mind.

CHAPTER SIX

Monday, June 27, Night

The phone rang with an insistence Don didn't like. He'd just popped his fifth beer, and after once again thumbing through his 300+ channels, had finally found something worth watching, maybe.

"Damn," he said, climbing out of the warm welcoming leather of his favorite recliner, and trudging across the family room, his hand wrapped around the neck of the beer bottle he took with him.

Don's, "Yes?" was crisp and completely sober.

"Don. It's Bobby."

"Oh. Hey there Bobs. Wha's up?" Don said, the slur slipping in along with relief that it wasn't work calling him in for another long shift.

"I know this is kind of a strange question but, have

you seen Julie?"

"Your wife, Julie?"

"Well sure," said Bobby, a little surprised by the question, but beginning to realize that Don was drinking, again.

Don took a long draw on the bottle and thought the question through. "Uh no. Not today anyway. Why?"

"It's getting kind of late and she hasn't shown up at home yet."

"Probably had to go somewhere," Don said reasonably.

"Sure, but it's not like her to forget to leave a note."

"Probably some teachery thing," Don continued, as if he was talking to himself. You check the school? Tha's what I'd do. I'd check the school."

Bobby, finally realized that his friend and coworker was too far in the bottle to be of much help. "Can you ask Barb if she's seen Julie?" he asked, speaking slowly and clearly.

"Sure, if she ever gets home. Hey, maybe that's where she is, hanging out with Julie. You should maybe call the gym."

"That's a good idea. Thanks."

"No trouble at all," said Don and tried to hang up the phone. It took him two tries because the cradle was small and tricky. Barb and Julie. Yeah, that's where they were. The gym. Where the hell else would Barb be?

Don staggered back to his recliner and fell into its soft embrace. The television screen flickered with the images of a bow hunter and a herd of elk, but he wasn't paying attention anymore. Don's thoughts had drifted from Bob's wife, to his own.

Barb. Damn, she'd been so pretty. First time he'd seen her she was in a white linen sun dress standing in the backyard of Judge Butcher's house. She was tall and slender and had the unselfconscious poise and posture of a dancer. As he wove through the crowd toward her he'd had to remind himself several times that he was self-confident, charming and that she'd be flattered by his attention. Despite all the self-talk, he found he was incredibly nervous as he introduced himself. Luckily, despite the stammering and nerves, Barb had been easy to talk to, and he soon found himself telling jokes that she actually laughed at. Her laugh was like a warm shower on a cold day. He wanted to keep her laughing and even came up with a pretty clever one based on Judge

Butcher's last name. It wasn't until later that night, when a new assistant district attorney was introduced to her, that he learned that Barb was the Judge's daughter.

They still laughed about that. She'd been something special back then: kind, funny and classy. If he'd made a list of the sort of wife he wanted, the perfect wife for a man with ambition, she'd have been it. She would never embarrass him. She'd never answer the door in a moth-eaten housecoat, or forget to comb her hair, or send her kids off with peanut butter and mayonnaise sandwiches because she was too drunk to tell mayonnaise from jelly, like his dear mother.

Don belched and reached down for the last beer in the cardboard holder sitting on the floor next to his chair. The bottle was wet with condensation and not as cool as he'd like. Still, it was beer. He twisted the top off and tossed it toward a decorative bowl of seashells and driftwood from trips collected on vacations to the beach. The cap missed the bowl, spun off the coffee table, and landed somewhere on the floor. Don sighed heavily and wished Barb was home. He wasn't ready to give up. Not yet. If Barb was here he'd take her into the bedroom and make love to her all night long.

He couldn't remember the last time they'd been together. Nah, that wasn't true. It was that night after he'd gone to see her play the last tennis match of the season. She'd won of course; she almost always won. To celebrate they'd stopped at Main Street Tavern where he'd had a couple beers and she'd had several glasses of white wine.

Afterward they'd gone home. Before he had the front door completely shut she was all over him. She tossed his hat across the room, ripped a button off one of his favorite shirts, and dug her nails into his skin as she tried to unbutton his jeans. Some guys might like that kind of aggression but he found it pushy and unfeminine.

Once he'd slowed her down enough to get her in bed things had been better. He was physically bigger and stronger and it didn't take that much effort to get her on her back, pin her arms above her head. He'd taken her roughly, wanting maybe to hurt her, just a little. But instead of making her submissive, it had made her crazy hot.

Before he could get back in control she'd slid out from under him and climbed on top. She tossed her head and the lights from the street made the blond strands glisten. It was okay, he decided. What man wouldn't envy him; having a pretty woman like his wife bucking up and down, her hair wild, her head thrown back, eyes closed? Her tits were a little bit small, but firm like a young girl's, her stomach was flat, her skin unbelievably soft. He took his hands from her belly and then slid them up her legs, from her knees, along the top of her thighs. He felt her taut skin, moist with exertion, her muscles bunching, flexing, hard as cable under his hands.

It reminded him of that time, up in the bleachers, when Coach Fry had trapped his hand against his thigh. The coach had moved his leg and Donnie felt the muscle under his hand, corded muscle, hard and warm. He jerked his hand away like it had been burned. Coach had coughed to cover up his embarrassment, making out like it was an accident. Only Donnie knew, even if he pretended, that it had been no accident.

Soon after, Donnie started making everyone call him Don. He also joined the sheriff's cadet program. Not much time for sports anymore. He didn't even play football his last year of high school or go out for track either. Sure, he liked to run, but he preferred competing against his own time. At least that's what he told himself.

All those memories cluttering up his thoughts had made him lose interest in sex.

"What's up?" Barb had asked when she realized his condition, then jokingly, "Or should I say down?"

He pushed her away, swung his legs to the side of the bed and sat up. "Too damn much beer I guess."

"Well it happens."

"Never happened before." She touched his back and it made him jump.

"Sheesh, you're awful twitchy."

"Just work. Lots of stress. Coming up for review in a couple weeks. You know."

"Yeah," she said, stifling a yawn. "Work sucks. Come back to bed. We can play tomorrow."

"Gotta get rid of this beer first."

"Mmmm," she mumbled, falling back against her pillow, her hand leaving a trail of goose flesh along his side.

The next morning, when his alarm went off, he found she'd already gone. He wondered if she would tell anyone about how he couldn't get it up. No, she wouldn't do that. What was he thinking?

They hadn't had sex since. Not her fault. She'd tried

to get him interested, but either he was too tired or he was heading out the door and there just wasn't time. Last night she'd reminded him that it had been almost three months. He couldn't believe it.

"Three months," he mumbled, draining the last of the warm beer and then fumbling to put it back into the container with the rest. "Three . . . "

He passed out with his hand still wrapped around the last beer bottle.

CHAPTER SEVEN

Wednesday, June 29, Morning

On Wednesday morning Don showed up for work all spit and polish. Chuck was aware of this fact because he was parked on the fifth floor of the parking structure across the street from the Law Enforcement Center. There was nothing to block his view but three steel cables strung across the opening—so basically, nothing.

The Law Enforcement Center, which everyone who worked there called the LEC, housed the county jail, the office where folks lined up to pay their parking tickets, and the Sheriff's Office.

Chuck's panoramic view afforded a direct line of sight of the front door, the well-groomed rectangles of lawn, the ugly as hell kinetic sculptures that turned erratically at the slightest breeze, and the rows of concrete barriers put in place after 9/11. It also allowed him to see who came and went.

This was exactly how Chuck had found the first woman to pay for his beloved Beverly's death. He'd followed that moon-pie faced kid as he left work a few times. Sure enough, eventually he'd led Chuck right to his front door. From there it had been simple for Chuck to park nearby and wait for a time when the kid was gone and the wife home.

His original plan had been to take her there at her house, but that day she'd left right after her husband. He'd been annoyed, but after waiting a heartbeat he followed her. She drove straight to an elementary school, drove across the teacher lot in the front and around to the back. He stayed back, waited a few minutes and then followed.

Her car was parked near a set of back doors. It was empty. She must have gone inside. He found a place to park nearby and looked around. They were behind three stories of brick and concrete that would block any view from the street. The rest of the lot was surrounded by a wide hedge at least seven feet tall. It conveniently blocked the view of the nearby houses. Or, more accurately, it blocked the view of the rather plain architecture of the school from the view of those living in the upscale neighborhood that surrounded it. At least that's what he believed, but whatever the reason for the hedge, it didn't really matter. What mattered was luck, and it was all his.

Unbuckling his seat belt and rolling his shoulders he settled in to wait. It was a short wait. In less than half an hour the little blonde came out to her car, her arms loaded down with boxes. A few quick steps, a gentle tap with the club and down she went. Hell, she'd been smiling at him. Probably thought he was hurrying to give her a hand.

Sitting there in the parking garage, thinking about her pretty smile, made him regret anew his reluctance to take a little spin before tossing her in the truck. Sighing, he rolled his eyes to the right. Nope. No Beverly. She'd been quiet today, a blessed relief.

Wrapping his hands around the end of his binoculars so that the lenses would be in shadow, less likely to flash and give away his position, he got back to scanning the front of the building. He had a window cracked and would hear the elevator or a car long before either one could make an appearance. If someone did show up he'd pretend to scribble into a notebook, try to look like he was calculating a bid or something.

The van had been a stroke of genius. White vans were everywhere. Sure, there was an old joke about them being the first choice of killers, but hell, there was a good reason for that. Slap a sign on the side and they became damn near invisible. He could sit here all day, his lunch pail full of sandwiches, his thermos full of coffee. When nature called, there was even a nice little cafe on the first floor that he could use for the cost of a muffin. Damn, it was good to be invisible.

Too bad for the cops that they weren't. So far he'd spotted the moon-faced kid and the one whose name had been on the ticket, Officer Don Giggler. He'd yet to see the third one, the one he thought of as blue eyes. He could still remember those eyes, that same blue so many artists used to paint shadows on snow. That was a cold color and a cold man. He'd never forget what they'd done to his Beverly. Never forgive them.

"Oh, Honey you still care."

"Of course," he told her, lowering the binoculars to

his lap and giving her his best smile. She smiled back, then reached up to adjust the combs in her hair. She had such long, beautiful hair.

He'd been so busy admiring Bev that he almost missed Giggler coming out of the building. Luckily he'd caught him from the corner of his eye. He was heading for his patrol car parked at the curb. Chuck hurriedly started the van and with tires squealing, sped as fast as he dared down the several looping stories of parking structure.

He reached the street and slowed. Bent over the wheel he looked left. Nothing. Then he looked to his right. A white car with a light rack on top and Eulalona Sheriff spelled out in big, black letters was sitting at a stop sign. Had the kid made a U turn? He was pointing the opposite way. Or was this someone else? Should he go left or right? He decided to follow the car he had in sight. If he was wrong it wasn't the end of the world. Having made a decision, he immediately felt more relaxed.

"I think you're making the right choice," said Bev. *"That's probably him."*

"I hope so," said Chuck. "Be nice to get this over quick and head back home."

"Wish I could go home with you."

"You will honey. You'll be with me no matter what. You know that."

Bev smiled her contented smile and sat back. Chuck pulled out of the parking garage and turned right.

Without much traffic to hide behind, Chuck fell back and let the van blend with other work vehicles. Then his prey turned onto a narrow, one way side street and things got a little tougher. Chuck looked around and saw that they had entered a neighborhood of smaller mid-century homes. The neighborhood appeared to be laid out in a grid pattern. It might be a good idea to turn and catch a parallel street. Keeping an eye on the car that way would mean less chance of being noticed. Of course, that wouldn't work so well if the street was a one way going the wrong direction. A few seconds went by as Chuck tried to make up his mind, but then the decision was taken from him.

The patrol car unexpectedly pulled into the driveway of a small white house set deep in its lot. A row of lilacs bordered the edge of the driveway, stretching from the street to the corner of a small, one-car garage. Past their season, a few dying clusters of dark purple flowers still hung, nodding in the light breeze. Chuck drove past the house, stealing glances in his side view mirror. He heard the rumble of a garage door and the police car slid past the row of lilacs and into the garage. A moment later there was another rumble and a thump as the door closed. Chuck decided he was driving too slowly. He pressed down on the accelerator, speeding up to twenty-five. After a few blocks he circled back, drove up the street, and boldly pulled into a driveway diagonally across from the white house. He got out of the car, walked to the front door of the strange house, and knocked. He wasn't surprised when no one answered. These days everybody worked. The neighborhood was quiet as a tomb.

He checked the number, looked around as if puzzled—Bev would be proud of his attention to detail and his acting chops—then he climbed back in his van as if to wait. To sell it, he even pulled back the cuff of his sleeve and pretended to look at his watch.

He'd barely shut the door when he spotted a blue Mazda Miata coming down the street. It slowed, then pulled in at the house he was watching. A woman climbed out, smoothed the front of her skirt, reached into the car for her purse. She had long loose, curly brown hair and some nice curves, a bit too much hip for Chuck's taste, but her high-heels showed off some nice legs. He recognized her immediately. After all, he'd seen her every morning on his stake out of the Sheriff's Office. She was always one of the first to arrive. He'd pegged her as a secretary or receptionist, maybe an accountant.

Chuck licked his lips as he watched her walk toward the front door. He still wasn't sure this was his guy he'd followed. He hoped he'd come to the door, but no such luck. Maybe he should get out and scout around the house, see if he could catch a peek through a window.

"He's a policeman," Bev reminded him. *"He might see you, and he has a gun."*

Chuck sighed. "I know that, darling. I was just tossing the thought around. I wasn't really going to get out.

"Patience is a virtue," Bev reminded him.

Chuck had no response. He knew she was right.

Inside, Lauren found her house was dark. Don had pulled the curtains over the dining room slider. Thick and insulated they effectively blocked the light, and the view from prying eyes.

"Babe," he said, "thought you'd never get here."

Lauren smiled at the hungry growl of his voice. Sometimes she felt so guilty, letting herself get into a relationship with a married man. It was so dirty and cheap, all the things everyone said about it. But it was also exciting and Don was so ... so amazing. She wasn't sure where it was going but maybe somewhere, someday. If she didn't ask she wouldn't know. She could continue to pretend there was a future for her and not just a few sweaty hours followed by pangs of guilt and depression.

Don had already removed his holster, and all the other tools and gadgets, including his radio, which now lay on her kitchen counter. The volume was so low she could barely make out a fuzzy sort of hum and sometimes a word or two. He'd stripped down to his t-shirt and boxers and now turned his attention to taking off her clothes. He was uncharacteristically careful—she had to return to work looking none the worse for wear—but he was methodical too, and quick. They didn't have much time. They never did.

He unbuttoned her blouse, slid it off her shoulders and draped it across the back of a chair. She undid her skirt, stepped out of it off and handed it to him. He put it on the chair near her blouse. Now she wore only a thin slip, a lacy bra, lipstick, red two-inch heels, and his surprise. Giving him a seductive smile, she ever so slowly lifted her slip, drawing the silky fabric up, the lacy trim tickling her thighs as she revealed old-fashioned lace garters and hose, and an utter lack of panties.

By way of showing his appreciation they never made it to the bedroom. They made love on her nubby gold couch, finishing with time to spare.

"That was wonderful," she said, meaning every word.

"But a little fast," he apologized.

She shrugged, then giggled, "Not too fast."

They were lying on their sides, stretched out on the narrow couch. He wrapped his arm around her waist, pulled her close against him. She was warm and smelled wonderful, like exotic flowers. She sighed and snuggled closer. These moments were too short. He lifted a few damp strands of hair from her neck, gently bit her ear lobe.

"Mmm. Better not start," she warned him. "How's work today? Has it been busy?" Her questions were meant to distract him and they did.

"No busier than usual. Bobby called twice. Sheriff's got an APB out for Julie and put Bobby on leave."

"On leave? How come? He didn't do anything wrong."

"Paid leave," he amended. "He's spending all his time looking for his wife. No way he can pay attention and do the job. Better for him. Better for the department."

Lauren shrugged. "I guess that makes sense. If your wife was missing you wouldn't be in any shape to work either."

There was an awkward silence and Lauren wondered if her small fishing expedition wasn't about to backfire. Then Don sighed and cupped one of her breasts. "I don't know that I'd miss her all that much."

"You are sooo bad," Lauren said, rolling her hips against him and encouraging him as he thumbed her nipple.

"One more time?" he asked squeezing her breast hard.

She groaned as his nails dug in and his teeth grazed her shoulder. "O-oh yes," she agreed.

About an hour after Chuck parked the van, the front door he'd been watching opened and the woman reappeared. Chuck watched her close the front door, walk to her car, toss her purse onto the passenger seat, smooth her skirt and get in. She backed the car out, her expression completely neutral. A few minutes later the garage door rolled open and the Eulalona County car backed out. As the car neared the road the driver looked in the rearview. Chuck recognized the face and smiled.

"Now what do you think of that?" he asked Bev. Our Officer Giggler seems to have himself a girlfriend. Which do you think he likes the best, the brunette mistress or the blond wife?"

Bev said nothing.

"No, you're right, it's dumb to try and guess. We'll just have to add the slutty secretary to our list."

CHAPTER EIGHT

Saturday, July 2,Morning

They'd agreed to meet at the Starbucks on Main and Third. The coffee shop, close to both city and county offices, had become the morning hangout for local police and deputies who were caffeine addicted and willing to pay for it. Kayla and Stenn were the last to arrive.

Stepping into the shop, Kayla's mood immediately lifted. There was something soothing in the woodland greens and browns and the mingled scents of roasted coffee, cinnamon and caramel. The growl and hiss of coffee being ground and milk being steamed added an upbeat soundtrack. It reminded her of coming to work back when she was a cop, stopping in every morning before work. Usually she'd run into someone she knew and they'd chat for a few minutes. It had been a nice tradition. She hadn't kept it up since leaving the department. There had been too many awkward moments.

It was Saturday, but not as busy as she'd expected. Bobby, Don and Barb had already bought drinks and managed to grab the best seating area in the place, a corner in the back where a brown leather couch and three club chairs were arranged around a gas fireplace.

Kayla noticed that Don and Barb sat on opposite ends of the couch, while Bobby was slumped in one of the chairs, as boneless as a teenager. Kayla gave Stenn her coffee preference and went to join the others.

Originally Bobby had asked them to meet at his house, but the thought of talking about Julie's disappearance within the walls of her home had made everyone uncomfortable.

Kayla dropped her purse in one chair to save it for Stenn and took the one next to Bobby. Curious about how he was dealing with his wife's disappearance, she couldn't help glancing at him. He was out of uniform and his street clothes were disheveled. He looked as if he'd slept in them—if he'd slept at all. His eyes were red and there were dark circles under them. She noticed that he hadn't shaved. The untrimmed white-blond beard gave him a rougher appearance than she was used to. This wasn't the tidy, cheerful man she remembered. *If Stenn disappeared how would I change? Would I look this broken?*

Bobby sat up and cleared his throat.

"I appreciate you guys showing up," he said just as Stenn joined them. Kayla took the caramel latte he handed her then moved her purse so he could sit down.

"Of course," said Don, "Whatever you need from us."

There was an uncomfortable silence, broken when Stenn asked more pointedly, "What do you need?"

"I need you to help me find Julie," Bobby said, scowl lines deepening as if he were annoyed by the question.

"How?" asked Don. "The whole department is looking for her. The cities. The staters. What can we do that they can't?"

Bobby shrugged. "I don't know. But maybe . . . I don't know."

More silence, and again Stenn took lead. "Well, we could at least go over what we know. Maybe just talking about it will help us come up with some ideas.

"Sure," agreed Don, "It's worth a try."

"Wait," said Kayla. "I want to write this all down. That way we won't forget something, or have to go over it a hundred times." She dug in her purse and found a pen.

"I can tell you've gone to a few meetings," said Barb, with a tentative smile. "Here, will this help?" She pulled a spiral bound notepad from her purse and leaned forward to pass it across the slate-topped coffee table.

Kayla took the notepad and smiled her thanks. Barb nodded and sat back in her seat. She looked ill at ease and it wasn't hard for Kayla to imagine how awkward she must feel, the only one in the group who had never been a cop. Besides, the atmosphere was so grim it was nearly funereal, so even the simple act of smiling seemed wrong, a giant social gaff. She would have to try and make Barb feel welcomed. She owed her that much.

After the accident, she'd been too shy to go back to the gym and Barb had agreed to special training hours. That way she could come in while the gym was closed to the public and avoid the curious stares. Barb had been understanding and hadn't laid on the pity either. It was obvious she and Don were going through some sort of rough patch. Kayla hated to be nosy, but it was impossible to miss the distance between them, both the physical distance—they were sitting on opposite ends of the couch—and the lack of eye contact. It was as if they couldn't even look at each other.

Barb had mentioned a few things, mostly in a joking, slightly exasperated way, such as Don was always tired or angry about his job and sometimes hard to reach.

Kayla had figured Barb was venting some anger and frustration with someone safe, but she'd hoped they were getting past it. It sure didn't look like it. Sighing she tried not to think about it. It was, after all, their lives. All she could do was be a friend to both of them, listen and try not to judge or take sides. She didn't want Barb's infrequent complaints to color her own feelings for Don. They got along fine. Hadn't he come to her rescue just a few days ago? She hated how complicated things were.

Bobby sat up, scratched at his beard and said, "We didn't have a fight. Already told the detectives that. As far as I know no one fought with Julie about anything. No one hated her, or even disliked her. There's no obvious suspect. I'm thinking it had to be something random, some sort of—"

"Just the facts, Bobby. Stick with the facts," said Don. He leaned on the arm of the couch, all his attention on

Bobby. He had the dark-eyed focus of a shark looking at something it was about to swallow whole. Kayla respected his intensity but was concerned by how he sat twisted almost sideways, his back to Barb, effectively cutting her out. Barb did nothing to bridge the gap. Her body language was one of avoidance, one leg drawn up under her, her arms crossed, gazing on anything or anyone but Don.

As hard as it was to see her friends dealing with a troubled relationship, Kayla knew the only important thing was finding Julie. With notepad and pen at the ready she nodded to Bobby to continue.

Bobby took a deep breath and said, "I got home and she wasn't there. I thought she would be because it was her first day of summer vacation. School was finished for the summer. I decided to do some housework to kill time while I waited for her to get home. After a couple hours I called and it rang awhile, and then dumped me into voice mail. I tried a few more times."

Bobby didn't share that he'd hit redial, heard her voice, hung up, hit redial over and over. *Even while he was doing it he thought it was strange, but there was this feeling. A sense that something was wrong.*

"Then you went to the school," Stenn offered.

"Yeah, I-I." Bobby looked up and blinked a few times, quickly. "I found Julie's car in the back lot. It was the only one there. The passenger side door was open and a couple cardboard boxes were on the ground next to it. One had opened up and the papers that had been in it were scattered all over the parking area."

The memory of pieces of construction paper, artwork lovingly crafted by her first class of kiddos, all the bright colors thrown heedlessly to the ground, hurt in a way he couldn't explain.

"I called 911 and they dispatched a car, but I didn't wait. After I called the hospital and the urgent care clinic I got in my car and drove the nearest neighbor's. They hadn't seen or heard anything. No one had. I walked the whole neighborhood. It was the same thing every time. Either no one was home or the few people who were . . . " He shrugged.

"What happened when the unit got there?" asked Stenn

Bobby looked down and his face flushed. "They thought we should check the school. Said maybe she was still inside and someone had broken into her car. I felt like a jackass. Never thought of that. But I . . . " He looked up, his blue eyes flashing. "It gave me hope. I believed it. I had to. But she wasn't there."

Kayla could only imagine the pain that must have caused, that moment of reckless hope, only to have it torn away.

"Any chance she set all this up?" asked Don.

"Set it up?" said Bobby.

"Yeah, you know, made it look like she was kidnapped or something and just took off on you."

Bobby looked dumbfounded. "What kind of stupid idea—"

"Whoa, "I'm just exploring every avenue. That's what you want, right?"

Bobby nodded. Wrung his hands nervously. "Yes. But she'd never do that."

"Bobby's right," said Kayla, unable to sit quietly by." You know that, Don."

"Yeah, I know. I'm just trying to come up with something that makes sense."

"The only thing that makes sense," offered Stenn, "is that Julie was taken from her car by someone and is being kept from contacting Bobby. The only questions we should be asking ourselves are, who and why."

"Exactly," agreed Bobby. "But how do I find answers if I'm cut off? I can't believe they did that to me," he said, anger firming his voice.

"Best thing O'Neill could do," argued Stenn.

"What?" asked Bobby, his fingers tightening on the arms of his chair. Kayla expected him to lunge out of it any moment. "Keeping me out of things is the best thing?"

"Sure," said Stenn agreeably, "He knows you can act more freely this way and he knows you're tapped into every resource you need through us. He's on your side. You can bet on that."

Bobby sat back in his seat. Nodded thoughtfully.

"Maybe it was someone she knows," offered Kayla to get them back on track. "We should get a copy of her address book and calendar, maybe we'll see something the detectives won't."

"That's the smartest thing I've heard," said Bobby.

Stenn squeezed Kayla's shoulder. "Good idea," he agreed.

As the small group finally began to make some progress, the old man nursing his cup of black coffee and working a crossword puzzle at a table not far from their corner, ran through a mental list. He had them now, all of them and he knew what he had to do. To punish the three he had to deal with four women: a probation officer, a fitness coach, a receptionist and an elementary school teacher.

"Former teacher." Bev reminded him.

Flashes of memory; a white leg, red dust sifting down, the smell of exhaust, the sound of a shovel ringing against rock played in his head. Chuck nodded and said, "Yes, that's right, *former* teacher."

Ever since learning he had a girlfriend, Chuck had become fixated on Giggler. He'd parked near his house in the early hours, and followed him here this morning. When the rest of the group had shown up he couldn't believe the luck. No one looked at him twice as he got his coffee order and settled in, a stooped old man killing time. He bought a paper and worked the puzzle, wearing a frown of concentration as he strained to hear their conversation. It wasn't hard.

"Your hearing's as good as ever, isn't it dear?" asked Beverly.

"Damn right," Chuck said. "Good as the day I was

hatched." He realized he'd spoken out loud but didn't let it bother him. No one was surprised by an old man muttering to himself.

Carefully, without seeming to stare, he studied the five of them. He'd already known who Don Giggler was married to. A quick Google search at the library using Don's name and the name of the town had turned up an old announcement of Don's wedding to one Barbara Butcher, daughter of a prominent judge turned state representative. Barbara Giggler (née Butcher) was one of those civic-minded people who show up frequently in local papers at one charity or another. She also won a lot of tennis awards and played on various co-ed sports teams, another way to earn local fame. The elegant blond at the far end of the couch was his wife. His girlfriend was the woman in the house with the lilac hedge. He already knew where to find her.

The moon-faced kid with the missing wife was Bobby. The woman he'd buried in the woods had called out that name when she was banging on the walls of the truck.

He heard the name Stenn twice and realized that had to be blue eye's name. It wouldn't take much to find an address. Hell, he could spend half an hour with the phone directory and get all the information he needed, assuming Stenn hadn't yet given up his land line, like the young people all seemed to be doing these days. His girlfriend was there too, an extra bonus. He wasn't sure of her name, Katie or Kylie, something like that. Didn't matter. Once he found Stenn's place he'd just stake it out until she made an appearance. She'd show up. They always did.

He decided to stay where he was and finish the puzzle. Then he had to write a letter. The paper had given him an idea. Punishing the cops by taking their women was justice, but it would be that much sweeter if they knew why. A letter to the editor would remind them.

He'd need more coffee.

CHAPTER NINE

Tuesday, July 5, Morning

Kayla sat in her office on Tuesday morning staring at her monitor. She'd finished a report, checked her court schedule and was now able to take a break and let her thoughts drift. She had been supposed to join in a search and rescue training over the weekend, but she felt funny leaving while Bobby's wife was still missing.

She'd been grateful to have Monday off for the Fourth, but hadn't felt like driving to the lake to watch the fireworks. Instead she'd spent the day catching up on errands and housework, and the evening watching a movie whose name she couldn't remember. Stenn had offered to come over, but she'd told him to stay home and spend time with his dad, who'd been released from the hospital.

A strand of hair tickled the side of her neck and she tucked it behind her ear. Probably time to schedule a haircut. With summer here something short and cool that took less time to fix in the morning would be nice. She also needed to get some new clothes. Thinking about such mundane things seemed strange and somehow selfish, given Julie's disappearance and Bobby's pain. But life went on despite the terrible things that sometimes happened; bills had to be paid, lawns had to be mowed. Time was relentless and life had to be lived.

She wished there was something more she could do to help. They'd hung those horrible have-you-seen-this-woman flyers all over town. Had anyone ever actually been found because of a flyer?

Well, at least she had no doubts that Bobby had loved Julie and would never hurt her. He'd been the first to leave their meeting and after he'd gone, Don, cop to the core, had shared what they'd all been avoiding, that the detectives would be calling Bobby in for a long chat soon. The implication, that Bobby was the prime suspect in his wife's disappearance, was not lost on any of them.

Pulling up a status report on Jeff Raye, or Spider as he liked to be called, showed that he'd been released. Just one more thing to worry about. She'd have to set up another meeting with him, make sure she had control this time. She could always request he be transferred off her case load. She'd considered it for all of five seconds. The minute her boss didn't think she could handle her clients was the minute she'd lose all respect. Kayla would rather put up with Spider than let anyone believe she was afraid of him.

"How you doing?" Diana asked, poking her head into the office, but standing in the hallway as if reluctant to be pulled inside.

"Doing fine," said Kayla.

"Awesome. Well gotta run. Judge Sandoval in about fifteen minutes. Catch you later?"

"Sounds good."

Kayla's cell phone rang and she fumbled it out of the side pocket of her purse, which she'd stuffed in a bottom file drawer of her desk.

"Yes. Hello." she said into the receiver.

"It's me," said Stenn. "Dad's back in the hospital. They think it's his heart again. Can you meet me there?"

"Of course, I'll be there in half an hour."

"Good. About the same for me. Meet me at the ICU

waiting room, and thanks."

Kayla made quick calls to the clients with whom she had appointments, asking them to reschedule. Then she sent an email to her boss letting her know she'd cleared her schedule and needed to leave. Fifteen minutes from the time Stenn called she was backing her Jeep out of the parking lot.

From his lookout behind an old shack and rusted grain silo that he'd found conveniently located across the highway from the entrance of the Lehrer Ranch, Chuck watched Stenn's truck bump from the gravel driveway to the paved road and speed up. He wasn't burning rubber but he wasn't lollygagging either. Chuck started the van, waited a beat, then pulled out to follow.

The Lehrer place was on the northwest side of the valley, an area of low rolling hay fields and winter pasture shared by several ranches. In the distance, in every direction, humpbacked hills dotted with sage rose toward larger mountains, their jagged sage and pine topped summits touching the wind shredded clouds.

Chuck felt smug about how quick and easy it had been to find a Stenn in the skinny phone book and from there his last name. "The alphabet's a wonderful thing," he'd said to Beverly. The universe, obviously wanting to save Chuck from making a mistake, had made sure there was a big wrought iron sign at the entrance to the property that spelled out Lehrer in fancy script. Sometimes Chuck thought the whole thing was too easy, but mostly he just thought the cops he was following were young and dumb as dirt.

The truck was easy to follow, a big Ford F250 painted dark burgundy, but caked with light colored clay soil up past the wheel wells. Bits of chaff from straw or hay floated from the back of it, bouncing along the side of the road, sometimes ticking at the window of the van.

"Where do you suppose he's going?" asked Bev.

Chuck shrugged. "Couldn't say. Not yet noon. Maybe a hot lunch date? Whatever it is, he sure doesn't want to miss it."

"I can see that," said Bev. *I thought we agreed you'd go after that receptionist slut next."*

"Now honey, we never agreed on any such thing. I said I'd follow them and whichever gave me the cleanest opportunity would be the one I'd get next. And just what kind of language was that?"

Bev had the grace to blush, but then she'd always had that innate sense of good taste, another trait that he loved. *I don't know why I used that word. I guess the idea of a woman fooling around like that. Well, it's just wrong. Married people make a commitment when they say, I do."*

"They do indeed," he agreed, stopping just short of reaching across to pat her knee. He knew from past experience that his hand would pass right through to the woven seat cover. The sensation was disturbing.

Marriage. That was a hell of a thing. Never would have thought he'd end up married. Didn't think he was the type. He liked sex just fine, and having a woman around steady seemed like a good way to have sex, but marriage was a lot more than that. You had to feed them, buy them a house, hell even give them kids. The whole thing seemed like a bad idea. Then he'd met Beverly.

She was a teacher at a school for natives in a remote part of Alaska. He'd retired from the Navy and taken a job driving the truck that brought supplies to the schools, a refrigerated truck. Thinking about it now he did so love the irony. He'd back in to the freight dock, roll up the back door and start hauling out boxes of turkey wieners, skinless chicken, beef patties, frozen cookie dough, and gallons of milk. He was always a little surprised at how much milk and cookies a school required.

"I think he's turning," cautioned Bev.

"Thought he was heading into town," said Chuck as he watched the truck's distant rear lights disappear and then reappear as it rounded a curve. "Yeah, that's what he's doing, he was just going around a corner." Despite that, Chuck brought the van up a little closer.

They tore through town. Chuck was forced to run a yellow light more than once, and increasingly worried that Stenn would notice him. Finally, the truck turned off the highway onto a street that led up past clusters of medical and dental offices to the top of a hill and a new, multistoried, red stone and cedar building with a sign, Melvin Morgan Memorial Hospital.

Something must have happened, thought Chuck. Someone hurt or injured maybe. Could it be Julie? Had she survived somehow and dug herself free?

"That's not possible," Bev, reassured him. *"Once you kill them, they stay dead. You know that."*

Even the slightly chiding tone she took didn't annoy him. After all, she was right. The knot between his shoulder blades eased as he drove past the truck, which was pulling into a parking space, and continued around the building. If someone was hurt, then blue eyes would have his mind on that and not on whether someone was following him. Chuck found a spot to park and trotted back. By the time he arrived Stenn was gone.

He hurried inside and to the elevators, just missing the closing door. Shit. The arrow above the door was lit up but there were no indicators showing what floor it was going to. Maybe it was time to give up and head over to the receptionist's house. Bev would approve.

Gotta think. Stenn had been in an all fire hurry to get here, but he hadn't gone to the emergency room. That meant whoever he had come to see was checked in. If there was that much hurry the person was either going to have a baby, get emergency surgery or was in the ICU. The elevator doors opened and Chuck stepped inside. A directory was posted just above the floor buttons. Chuck took a gamble, found the ICU, stepped into the elevator and hit the appropriate button.

When the bell dinged and the doors opened he stepped out onto the fourth floor and almost ran into Stenn, who was pacing back and forth talking into a cell phone. Ignoring the mumbled, "Sorry, excuse me." Chuck brushed past and kept walking.

He found that they were in a long hallway that stretched along an outer wall made up mostly of glass. It served as a waiting room for visitors to the ICU. The view of the sage-covered hills and the wide sweep of sky was noteworthy, but Chuck didn't have time to dawdle. At the end of the hall was a set of double doors marked Staff Only.

He thought about going through, but if someone saw him it could cause a ruckus and draw attention. Noticing that a long row of benches lined the glass wall, Chuck took a seat at the far end, leaned back against the sun-warmed metal rail, whose purpose was probably to keep grubby hands off the glass, and picked up a magazine from a stack of them. He held the magazine in front of his face until Stenn was buzzed into the ICU. He glanced at his watch. He'd give it two hours.

He had been following Stenn, hoping he'd be able to follow him to his girlfriend's house. Once he knew where she lived the rest would be easy. He had hoped the woman lived with him, but only two names were listed in the phone directory for the Lehrer ranch, Lars and Stenn.

The only women he'd seen on the place were a short, heavy Hispanic woman, too old to be the cop's woman, and a girl that was probably her daughter or granddaughter, too young to be a candidate.

Maybe the girlfriend didn't like driving all the way out to the ranch. Maybe Stenn drove to her place to see her, like Don did to see his girl. If that was true, then maybe he'd go straight there from here. As much as Chuck hated the idea of wasting more time with all the waiting, watching and following, he knew there was no better way. He was angry, but he was also smart and very cautious. Settling down to practice patience, he held a whispered conversation with Beverly to kill the time.

Over the next hour a few people came through, an elderly couple; a young woman shedding tears, dressed in a skirt that was far too short; a trio of unsmiling teenagers with black boots and spiked collars; two doctors in green scrubs animatedly arguing baseball scores; an earnest young woman in jeans and a gray sweater; and a middle-aged woman wearing a cowboy hat, carrying a giant bag of yarn.

The woman in jeans and sweater accompanied Stenn when he came out of the ICU. Chuck had been half dozing and he stayed where he was. Better to look like an old fart catching a snooze than to try and hide his face with the paper again. He let his eyelids droop.

They seemed to be arguing, though it was hard to tell since they were doing their best to keep their voices low. Fortunately, the acoustics of the hall brought their half whispers to him clearly.

"But I don't mind being here," said the woman he now recognized from the meeting at Starbucks.

"That's nice but there's no need. I thought it was a bad one but it turns out it wasn't even a heart attack, more like indigestion. Dad keeps getting Carmen to make him spicy food, and gets Ray to sneak it to him, even though he knows it makes him feel like this. They gave him something for anxiety and it knocked him out. He's sleeping hard, but that's all. They're going to move him out of ICU and put him in a regular room, just to keep an eye on him for another couple of days. I'll hang around until they get him moved. He's anxious enough. When he wakes up in a strange room, I should be there."

"You should," she agreed. "You want company?"

"Are you sure? Hospitals are boring places."

Chuck peeked through his eyelashes and saw they

were standing face to face, the woman's anxious eyes focused on the cop. It was obvious she cared about him. Chuck hoped he cared as much for her. That way when she died it would hurt. He wanted those cops to hurt.

"I'm sure," she said.

Chuck studied the woman more closely. She wore a light gray sweater with a pattern of black leaves over a white, button down blouse. The blouse was tucked into washed out jeans. On her feet were lightweight hiking shoes. She was slender but not slight. Her hair was dark auburn, shoulder length and held in a short ponytail. She was pretty, with big eyes, high cheekbones, full lips and a strong jawline. With a bit of makeup and the right clothes he thought she could be a real looker. He'd have no trouble recognizing her again.

In fact, now that he thought about it, worse come to worse if he lost track of her, it would be easy enough to arrange to see her again. If she was willing to hang around and provide company to the cop at a hospital, she'd surely be willing to attend a funeral. After all, how hard would it be to find an old man named Lehrer? Hospitals didn't normally hide patients.

As soon as the two wandered back into the waiting

room Chuck strode confidently through the Staff Only doors. Without hesitation, he walked past the nurse's station, glancing at the white board as he strode by. The name Lehrer, Lars followed by a room number were written on a line in thick black marker. The two nurses at the station didn't even look up from their computer screens. Long ago Chuck had learned that the appearance of confidence could open a lot of doors.

Luckily the room he wanted was directly ahead. A quick look inside told him the occupant was asleep, as expected. He stepped up to the bed and looked down at the resting form. The old man's face was tanned and creased. Each breath was slow, shallow. Chuck was certain he would have little trouble placing a pillow over the man's face and keeping it there as long as necessary.

He almost patted the man's arm, but restrained himself. No sense waking the old fella up just to celebrate having a plan B. Felt good though. Plan A was taking up a post in the hospital's main lobby. He doubted the cop's girlfriend would take a back way out. When she came through the lobby he'd get to his car quick and follow her to her home.

"But what if she gets to her car too fast?" asked Bev.

"What if you lose her?"

"Not a problem," he whispered, explaining Plan B. If I lose her I'll come back here and then I'll find her again—at the old man's funeral."

"*That doesn't seem right,*" lectured Bev. "*He's just a helpless old man.*"

"Oh for . . . Beverly, sometimes I sure do get sick of hearing you rattle on."

Bev stopped talking and sulked. This time Chuck didn't care. He had a lot on his mind. So much that he didn't notice the old man was staring at him through half-closed eyelids.

CHAPTER TEN

Wednesday, July 6, Noon

Don was drunk and enjoying it. He was kicked back on Lauren's couch with a beer in one hand and Lauren's hair wrapped in the other. She'd taken a rare half day off in the middle of the week so they could spend some time together, and they were spending it well. At the moment she was kneeling on the floor between his legs, doing one of the many things his dear wife preferred not to. Well, that wasn't completely true. Barb was willing, she was just too willing. "Too darn pushy," he groused, the words slurring.

"Hmm?" asked Lauren, pausing. Don patted her on the head. "You go on, honey. Wasn't talking to you."

Lauren stopped, sat back, was about to say something, no doubt going to complain about what he'd said, complain about something. Don grabbed her hair and pushed her back down toward his crotch, held her there. "Get busy," he snapped. She wrapped her mouth around him and he moaned and stroked her hair. "God, I love you Lauren. I love you. I'm going to divorce that bitch and move in. That okay with you? No, don't stop. Don't..."

After a few moments Don surfaced out of his alcohol and sex haze with a bad sensation rolling through his gut. Or maybe that was just the beer. He could hear water running in the bathroom and could imagine Lauren spitting into the sink and brushing her teeth. He felt like a rotten bastard. What was with forcing her like that? Seriously uncool. Saying he loved her? Jesus, that was even worse. What if she really did expect him to leave Barb? What if he told her he didn't have any such intention? Sure, she was fun; a nice, sweet woman with some real talent in bed, but what the hell would happen to his career if he divorced a judge's daughter and moved in with a secretary with a fat ass? The idea made him nauseous.

Groaning, he stood up and got dressed. He was still a little off kilter. Had to knock off the drinking, at least during the day. He found his jacket and managed to pull it on, found his keys, they jangled as he took them off the hallway table and the noise made him cringe. He felt guilty as hell. The Honda Civic, the ultimate car for men who don't have the balls to tell their wives that economy is not the best reason to choose a car, was safely stowed in Lauren's garage. At least he wasn't driving his patrol car. Getting seen here driving that was a real fear.

"What are you doing?" Lauren asked, concern putting a crease between her eyebrows and a pout on her freshly made up lips.

"Gettin' ready to go."

"You weren't going to leave without saying goodbye, were you?" she asked, the pout growing.

"Oh, hell no babe. Just getting my shit together. Was about to go look for you."

"You can't stay?" Lauren asked, her voice thick with disappointment.

I'm such an ass, Don thought. "You need me to help you out? I didn't mean to leave you hanging."

Lauren looked at him quizzically. Then, as understanding of his offer dawned on her, she stepped past him to the kitchen door that opened into the garage, flung it wide and smacked the button mounted on the wall. The garage door began rolling up. "There's your car. Better get it out of here before someone sees it," Lauren said in a soft voice, unnervingly at variance with the hard look in her eyes.

Not quite grasping her sudden shift in mood, Don was not so drunk that he thought hanging around was a good idea. "I'll call you." he promised, stepping past in that overly precise way of the practiced alcoholic. She slammed the door behind him.

An hour later, when the doorbell rang, Lauren was sure it was Don returning to apologize. She hadn't quite decided what attitude she'd take with him. She was hurt and angry, angry enough never to see him again? She didn't have the answer for that—yet. Maybe that was up to him. Would he be able to convince her to forgive him?

She opened the door, her face a carefully arranged mask. But it wasn't Don who stood there. It was an old man.

"Excuse me," he said. With his left hand he fumbled to remove his hat, an old fashioned but charming tradition when greeting a woman. She was so distracted by the gesture that she didn't see his right hand come up, the blackjack a blur. All she noticed was the tremendous shock and pain when it struck the side of her head and sent her reeling backward. He stepped inside, his foot shot out and he swept her legs out from under her. As she was falling, he pushed the door shut.

Lauren was in such shock and pain she couldn't think straight. She knew she was on the floor. The molding she'd taken such trouble to sand and paint white was at eye level. She could see a scuff mark and a spot where one of the nails hadn't been sunk deeply enough. It caused a little bump in the surface. The carpet was rough on her cheek.

The stranger rolled her onto her back, grabbed her wrists, and strapped them together with some sort of thin, plastic tie. She did nothing to stop him. Even when he grabbed her wrists and dragged her into the kitchen she couldn't manage the energy or will to fight. The movement made her feel sick to her stomach, and she was happy when it stopped. She stayed where he left her, face down on the linoleum staring at a wallpapered wall. The blurry image resolved into a small, red rooster, but though she could see it clearly she couldn't remember the name for rooster. There was something wrong, but she was too distracted to think about it much.

She heard the garage door closing. It was just like when Don came over. He couldn't be seen at her house of course. He was married. She was seeing a married man. That made her the other woman. She should be ashamed, but she was not. It was the first time in her life she felt like she was winning.

The man who had hit her and tied her up returned, distracting her from her thoughts about Don. He grabbed the slender strands of plastic around her wrists and pulled. It hurt and she didn't know what he wanted at first, but he was persistent, and very strong. Finally she understood and struggled to her feet, where she stood swaying, vertigo threatening to make her sick again. After a moment it receded and her mind cleared a bit. She was even able to lift her head.

"Come with me," the man said, tugging on her upper arm. He stepped toward the garage and she went along with him, sliding her feet, one after the other, as weak and trembling as her mother had been the last few days of her life.

Lauren wondered if this was what old felt like. She

thought so, either old, or like someone coming out of a long illness, weak and tired and something else, something wrong you can't quite put your finger on. Leaning against the doorjamb for a moment, she tried to gather her strength, organize her thoughts. Slowly she managed to navigate down the two stairs to the garage level. After that it was easier and she shuffled across the garage to the side of the van.

Van? Why was a van in her garage? She swallowed. Something was wrong. She'd opened the front door because Don had come back. Then something happened? An explosion? A tear rolled down her cheek. It was warm. She blinked. The gray shapes at the periphery of her vision pushed back. She was in her garage. There was a white van, so big, right in front of her. Why was a van in her garage? Someone was holding her arm. His fingers were digging into her skin.

The side door of the van slid open with a scratchy rumbly noise. The inside of the van was dark, but not too dark. She could see a shovel and other tools hanging from cords and beneath them a row of white plastic buckets all attached to the wall with bright blue cords. The color was bright against all that white. Pretty.

The man who held her arm tried to push her forward and into the van. There was a sleeping bag unrolled in front of the buckets. It looked soft.

"Sleeping bag," she mouthed. She knew what that was. Visions of camping trips with her mom and dad, her flirtatious cousins, they skipped through her thoughts, disjointed and out of order but there was a connection.

"Get in and climb in the bag," he told her. She understood his words better now and shook her head, no. That made her head ache more and she felt a warm, sticky something running behind her ear. He'd hit her. The old man had hit her with something and now he wanted her to go into the van.

Suddenly she jerked back, surprising both of them, broke free of his grasp, jumped the stairs and over the door sill into the kitchen where she spun, and with both bound hands clawed for the door knob, trying desperately to pull the door shut behind her, to lock the monster out.

His body crashed into hers, one arm wrapped around her neck. They both fell, she taking the brunt of the force, smashing her shoulder into the countertop and then crashing to the ground, his weight coming down hard on top of her. Her upraised arms kept her from hitting her head, but her knees and one elbow slammed into the floor. The pain was sharp and immediate, taking her breath away.

Before she could think, he'd rolled her onto her back and was straddling her, her arms trapped under his legs.

"Bitch." Chuck spat the word under his breath as he drew back his hand for another blow. He slapped her three times, as hard as he could but with an open hand. He didn't want to cause damage, just teach her a lesson.

Blood was trickling from her nose and he took a deep breath and leaned back. She winced, and turned her head aside, as if expecting him to strike again. He didn't. He just knelt and looked at her. Her dark hair was mussed. He reached up and smoothed it. Some of her blood got on his finger and he wiped it off on his pants. There wasn't much blood. She kept her face turned aside, her eyes down, didn't move. He liked that. Naturally submissive. He liked that a lot.

"She's a deputy's girlfriend," said Bev, out of nowhere.

Jesus, the woman's timing.

"I'm just trying to protect you. He might come back.

You know it's not safe here."

Chuck sighed, a heartfelt sigh that came clean from his boots. He reached into his back pocket and pulled out the blackjack he'd put there a bit prematurely. He held it in front of Lauren's face.

"Open your eyes. Open them now and look at what I've got."

Lauren looked. It took a moment to focus on the object in his hand but she had no trouble focusing on his words. "If you do what I tell you we'll get along fine, if you don't I'm going to smash your face in. I'll break your nose and your teeth and I promise you, your cop boyfriend will never want to touch you again. We clear? Nod if you understand."

Lauren did so, without hesitation. The tiniest of sounds came unbidden from her throat. She shut it down.

"I'm going to get to my feet and then you will get up. You will walk to the van in front of me. You'll climb into the van and into the sleeping bag. You'll put your head where the feet normally go. Do you understand?"

Lauren nodded, her eyes still fixed on the club he held an inch from her nose.

"Time to get up, girlie. Just bad luck for you that you're a cop's girlfriend."

"Cop's girlfriend?" Lauren muttered. "I'm a cop's girlfriend."

Chuck kicked her in the side. "Get up and get moving."

Lauren coughed; the sudden blow had taken her breath again. All she wanted was to lie there and inventory the pain in her body, but there was no other choice. She rolled to her hands and knees and laboriously got to her feet. Her entire body was trembling. Her head ached and her face burned where he'd slapped her. There was a sharp pain in one of her elbows and both of her knees throbbed. Tears trickled steadily down her cheeks. She tasted them on her lips.

Despite the tears, Lauren did not feel as shocked or fearful as she had earlier. A strange sort of calm had taken over. With a sort of eerie detachment, she watched as a woman who looked like her climbed into the van and lay down on the sleeping bag. Even though it was like watching someone on screen, the movie was so good she could feel what the woman was experiencing: the light from the overhead fluorescent reflecting off the gleaming side of the van hurting her eyes, the softness of the sleeping bag, the smell of perfume that was not hers. But those were physical things. It was her emotions that seemed absent, or if not absent, at least blunted, as if someone had sanded the sharpest edges away. *Is this what it feels like to be in shock she wondered*? But even that thought seemed far away and not terribly important.

The old man told her to lie on her back with her head in the narrow end of the sleeping bag. He put a wad of paper towels in her mouth and tied it in place with something made of cloth. As he zipped the sleeping bag closed, Lauren lost consciousness.

CHAPTER ELEVEN

Friday, July 8, Morning

Kayla chewed the end of her pencil, looked at her calendar, and tried to calculate the odds that Spider would come in for his appointment. Her friend Diana had put the odds of him showing up at 60 to 40. She figured he must know it would be a bad idea, after his last stunt, to do anything more to make his PO angry. Kayla wasn't sure he was that smart.

He'd spent Tuesday night in jail, but had been kicked out early because the jail had filled with people who had done more to earn the space. If he showed up, she'd have a serious conversation with him, outlining exactly what she expected of his future behavior. If he didn't, she'd fill out a warrant request, and see how he'd like to talk to a judge instead.

She was thanking God for Friday and pretending not to care. The problem was she did care. The idea that he'd show up and there would be another altercation made her stomach feel like she'd chugged a gallon of ice water. That icy weight in her gut, along with the sizzle of nerves that made her hands tremble, was part of that new and ever present friend, fear.

She'd tried to defeat it by distracting herself, analyzing the incident with Spider a dozen times and coming up with a dozen ways she could have handled it better. That hadn't really helped. You couldn't go back in time and fix a mistake, and it hadn't reduced her anxiety about dealing with him again. Maybe work was the answer, burying herself in the piles of work that were always waiting for her. She reached for the top file in her in-box.

When the phone rang, Kayla had been re-reading a report she'd typed into the computer, checking for any reference to emotion versus observable states. The court frowned on such descriptions as, "Mr. Smith came into my office in a bad mood." The approved narrative would read, "Mr. Smith came into my office and pounded his fist on the desk." Facts were observable. Emotions were not. At least that was the argument. Kayla wondered how objective or subjective an observation could be, even about observable behaviors. What if Mr. Smith was just trying to squash a bug with his fist?

The ringing phone ended her musings and her sense of relaxation. Spider had arrived.

While Kayla walked down the long hallway to get her client, Bobby Jones was still on the phone. He'd been given a copy of the pages from Julie's address book and had been calling, leaving voice mails when he couldn't reach someone. So far, no one had reporting seeing her since the day before she'd gone missing. All he could hope for was that someone he'd left a voice mail for would call with good news. Though the idea that she'd simply left him, was hiding out somewhere, was so absurd.

Still, he had to cling to any small hope he could find. If she had left him he'd be devastated, but if it was worse, he'd be destroyed.

He'd decided to call the hospitals again, this time asking about Jane Does matching her description and broadening the scope. There weren't many possibilities to run through. Maybe she'd been mugged. Taken somewhere and dumped. Maybe she was in a coma somewhere with no ID. After the hospitals, he'd call morgues and coroners. A friend at the office told him they'd already contacted the local coroner's office, and they'd promised to contact all the other offices in the state, but Bobby had been part of a bureaucracy long enough to know how faltering the lines of communications could be. He was leaving nothing to chance.

After a while Bobby got sick of his own voice. He had to get up, get out and do something before he lost his mind. He took his cell phone, making sure it was fully charged, and got into his car. First he went to the school where Julie's car had been found, driving slowly around the perimeter of the parking lot, not sure what he hoped to find. After that he drove the neighborhood, stopping at every store, every possible place she might have stopped. At each he took Julie's photo from his wallet and showed it to the shop owner or manager. "Have you seen this woman?"

"Why?"

"She's missing."

"Oh, that woman. Yeah. Someone from the Sheriff's Office already talked to me."

"Well now *I'm* talking to you."

"Yes sir."

Bobby didn't realize that there was a new look in his eyes, an uncompromising tone to his voice that made those he questioned uncomfortable and eager to answer. They wanted him to get what he needed and go. Bobby was only aware of a growing sense of time ticking by and a sense of panic, which seemed to take the place of more and more of the air in his lungs with every breath.

One of his stops was an office supply store. He had another two hundred copies of Julie's photo blown up and printed, adding his cell number and an offer of a reward for information. He knew Kayla and Barb had posted flyers. They were everywhere he'd gone that day, but what else could he do? He left them at every stop he made that morning.

Once he'd visited every store, laundromat and office he could find, Bobby returned to the school parking lot and sat in his car.

Don had a headache and his mouth felt like he'd been chewing his feather pillow all night. He kept thinking about Lauren and Barbara, Barbara and Lauren. He wanted both of them. He wanted neither of them. Maybe what he wanted was Coach Fry to put his hand on his leg so he could get a good and lasting boner. Jesus. He needed a drink, and a therapist, in that order.

He thought about calling Stenn. Reaching out like some loser in AA calling his sponsor. That's what it would have felt like, but he'd have done it, if Stenn was still a cop. Stenn being a hay farmer, that was wrong; that was just another example of the universe kicking you in the teeth. He didn't need more reminders. He needed a beer.

Maybe he should call Stenn's girlfriend. Kayla was easy to talk to. Closest to a woman friend he'd ever had. She'd probably tell him to quit screwing around, get his head on straight, fix his marriage and dump his girlfriend. Hell, that's what he'd tell someone in the same situation. Yeah, that's what she'd tell him to do. Kayla was cool.

Maybe if he'd met someone like that, someone uncomplicated, easy to talk to, easy to look at. Really fucked up, getting her foot blown off. It didn't show though. Just a little limp sometimes. Stairs were probably a bitch. Would it be weird to have sex with an amputee? You had to think about it. What would that feel like? He could imagine touching it, the feeling of it sliding along his side with him on top. Damn.

Adjusting himself, Don scanned the parking lot. Empty. Good. He coughed, self-consciously into his fist. Barb now, she'd be okay if she lost a leg. She was self-sufficient, tough as a guy. Lauren, she'd probably be a mess, too needy and emotional. Barb would never let someone help her, would keep her distance, while Lauren would need someone to take care of her. Hell of a choice. Which was better?

Somewhere down the row of cars a door slammed and Don unbuckled his seat belt, pulled the keys from the ignition.

What the hell was going on in his head? Was he really sitting here thinking about his best friend's woman? Developing some new kink? Christ. He should be sitting here thinking about what a great goddamn life he had. After all, he had Barbara, who loved him, kept a great home, was popular and connected in the way an ambitious career cop's wife should be, and he had Lauren.

Lauren was sexy and curvy and yielding. She probably wouldn't even be all that angry after that last fumbling, drunken stunt of his. She was good like that. With a little more attention and effort she might even go for some of the kinky shit. A ball gag maybe. Would look good with that red lipstick she liked to wear. Another visit to her place might be just the way for him to blow off steam, get his head back in the game. The idea of her back on her knees was appealing in a way that tented his pants. Damn what was wrong with him today?

He'd stop by Lauren's desk on the way in. Tell her he was sorry. Maybe ask her out to dinner. They'd go to that restaurant just over the county border where they'd gone once before. The food was decent and it was far enough out of town that they'd be unlikely to run into anyone they knew.

Maybe afterward, he could persuade her to drive up one of the logging roads. He'd have to remember to toss a blanket in the trunk. Funny, how he couldn't get it up for his wife, but had made love to Lauren every chance he got, even in the backseat of a car like a damned teenager. If he played it right, maybe he could even swing by her place today, do the old lunch thing again.

He had to block his thoughts with a long list of crime stats before he could casually climb from the car and walk toward the LEC.

"Hey," he said with a friendly smile to the receptionist, a tall, thin, wrinkled character who had to be in her late fifties or early sixties but wore dreadlocks and had a cluster of stars tattooed on her sagging neck. "Lauren around?"

The woman looked up at him with a knowing smirk. Inch-long, black nails stopped clattering against her keyboard as she gave him a thin smile and answered his question. "Well honey, wish I could answer that for you, but Miss Lauren didn't see the need to come in or call yesterday or today."

"That's not like her." said Don.

"Well, she hasn't done it before. All I know for sure is it's a good thing I showed up or the doors would still be locked."

"Okay, well thanks," muttered Don, suddenly uncomfortable under the gaze of this semi-stranger he'd walked past every day for the last three years.

"You want to leave a message, in case Lauren does decide to show up?"

"No. No thanks. Just wanted to ask her about a—a party my wife wanted to invite her to."

"Your wife?" the woman asked, arching an eyebrow.

"Yeah, my . . . my wife." It occurred to Don that he was talking to Lauren's coworker. Who knew what they talked about. "S-she runs these charity things," he stammered. "Well, I better get to work."

"Okay then. You have a good one."

"Thanks. You too." Don fled, walking slowly, but fleeing nonetheless. He could hear his over explanation playing over and over in his head as if it were on a loop.

Was this ever going to stop? Was he always going to feel like he was being ripped in half? Maybe he should just give up on women entirely. Go home and tell Barb he wanted a divorce. Find Lauren and tell her he wanted to break up. Hell, maybe she wasn't coming in to work because he'd upset her on Wednesday. He should probably go buy some flowers on his lunch break. Flowers could fix almost everything.

CHAPTER TWELVE

Friday, July 8, Afternoon

Spider walked ahead of Kayla, his shoulders rounded and telegraphing the abject attitude of a beaten dog. Kayla didn't buy it for a second. Where was the rage and violence? She was sure it was lurking not far below the surface. She was glad now that she'd moved her furniture. It was a bit awkward to sit with her back to the door, but it sure made access to the exit a lot simpler.

Settling into one of the chairs, Spider placed his hands in his lap and looked down at his feet. "I just want to say how sorry I am for last time. I don't know what made me to flip out like that."

"Had you taken anything?"

"You mean like drugs?"

Kayla sighed. "Yes, like drugs."

"No ma'am. I'm in recovery and I don't mess with that stuff no more."

"Of course. Look Spi . . . Mr. Raye. I don't for a minute believe you're in recovery. In fact I'm pretty sure the UA I'm about to ask you to give is going to come out as clean as the water in Diamond River."

"Ain't that the river that was in the paper? The one that takes the overflow from the factories and farmland?"

"That's right, they call it the fish killer. You think I'm wrong about your UA?"

"I think I'll pass just fine. Last time was just, I don't know. I got a temper sometimes. Maybe I need a counselor."

"You turned down a counselor. Are you saying you've changed your mind?"

"I guess, as long as I don't have to keep one permanent. I might change my mind again."

"I understand," said, Kayla. What she understood was that Spider would say whatever he thought she wanted to hear. There wasn't a sincere bone in his body.

"Look, let's be really clear. You have a short list of things you need to take care of and then you're off probation. I'll do everything I can to help you get through that list. I'm not here to be your enemy. I'm here to support you in staying out of prison. We really don't want you back. But that means you have to clean up your act. You need to tick off everything on that list and you have to stay out of trouble. That includes not bothering people, not playing stalker, not having angry confrontations with officers of the court or law enforcement or citizens. Do you hear what I'm saying?"

Spider nodded carefully. "I hear you. So, you're gonna hook me up with a counselor?"

Kayla sighed, "I'll see what I can do. For now let's go find a male PO and get that UA."

It was a relief to tell Spider he could leave as soon as he'd finished peeing in the plastic cup that a male co-worker would watch him fill. Spider struck Kayla as the kind of offender who would over fill the cup and then "accidentally" stumble and spill half of it on whoever was handy. In her frame of mind, if he did that to her he'd get badly mangled.

Kayla stood up, took the two short steps to the doorway planning to lead Spider out. Unfortunately one of those steps brought her foot into contact with a small, almost unnoticeable wrinkle in the carpet. Her foot turned and wham, she was flat on the floor. Almost as soon as she was down Kayla was fighting to get back up. She had to grab what she thought of as her bad leg, which had twisted and was now caught under her good leg. It was an awkward and embarrassing moment, especially with Spider there to witness it.

Roughly, she pulled her bad leg free. Spider, who had stepped back, shocked by her unexpected fall, now stepped forward and reached out to help. After the briefest hesitation, knowing a nearby coworker might show up at any moment, Kayla took his hands and let him pull her to her feet.

"Thanks," she said, and brushed herself off. "Caught my foot."

"I saw," Spider said.

Kayla realized he'd seen more than her fall, he'd also seen her prosthetic. Her pant leg had pulled up and revealed it. However he didn't say anything more and she was grateful for the unexpected courtesy.

"Let's go get that UA dealt with, okay."

"Sure," he said.

Returning to her office a few moments later, Kayla shut the door behind her and sank into her chair. It had been another bad moment. She counted them up like beads on a string. Stenn was worried about his dad. Bobby's wife Julie was still missing. She was pretty sure she'd smelled alcohol on Don when she ran into him on the stairs that morning. And of course, she'd still not completely accepted getting her foot shot off. She was a mess and so was everyone around her.

She'd believed that once she was done with college and entered the grown-up world, life would be easier. She'd hated almost every moment of high school where she was the quiet kid with acne being raised by that strange, quasi-hippy, semi-stoner aunt. A woman best known for throwing apples at neighborhood kids. Kayla knew she had zero chance at popularity. The best she could hope for, day to day, was a measure of invisibility.

College had been better, though she'd seen no need to be more visible and she'd found no real direction. She'd listened to her advisor and spent the first year taking a variety of courses, finding she liked sociology and psychology the best. She supposed it was her lack of understanding of people that made her interested in understanding them better. What she'd do with that, after she'd received four years of it, she had not a clue.

Luckily she didn't need one. A headhunter from the Sheriff's Office was there on career day and talked her into applying. With nothing better to do, Kayla had. She'd been surprised when a conditional offer of employment was made. All she had to do was pass cop school.

She'd attended the academy, learning that four years of college did not constitute a good training program. She'd struggled and then excelled at arrest procedures, close combat, firearms training, high speed driving and pursuit, and good old physical conditioning. The classroom stuff had been more painful. Her constitutional law class had left her weeping, and the entire report writing nightmare gave her a headache, but at the end of it she'd met the conditions and the offer was real.

After a two week break she'd gone to work and had loved everything about the job. Getting to drive the car, all the toys on her utility belt, practice at the gun range, the gun, the authority she had without having to ask, the people she worked with who really gave her a sense of being part of a family, and oddly the continuing physical training. Kayla loved the physical side of being a cop, the defensive training, taking down a bad guy. Unexpectedly, it was a rush.

In the beginning she'd been paired with a field training officer, Stenn Lehrer. Though she'd been attracted to him from day one, she'd been careful to keep her feelings to herself. You didn't date on the job. Less than a year later, and two and a half years into the job, she'd walked into that dark factory and changed her future.

Running her fingers through her hair, massaging her scalp to forestall a stress headache, Kayla tried to remember that she was lucky. Blue Spruce was slow recovering from the economic downturn. The whole county was barely limping along. She'd been fortunate to find a job as a probation officer after leaving the Sheriff's Office. She couldn't complain about that. It had been her choice. They'd offered her a desk job, even a chance to come back to active duty once her PT was done and she passed the physical, but she'd said no. She didn't want a desk job. Couldn't watch her friends go out every day while she was left behind. But that wasn't the truth, or at least not the whole truth. "You were such a liar," she said out loud in her empty office. "You were scared."

There, she'd said it. She left because she was scared. Still was. Even now there were nightmares she woke from, her skin slick with sweat, throat torn raw by a scream. In her recurring nightmares she moved through a world thick as gelatin while a monster's clawed hand tore her foot away its teeth clack, clack, clacking with an oddly oily snick, just like the sound of a shell jacking into a shotgun.

Shaking off the memory of her dark dreams, Kayla got up and opened the door to her office. Work. That's what she needed. Get busy and get her thoughts off the past.

Kayla was typing, her fingers flying across the keyboard when, sensing something, she turned in her chair to find Diane standing in the doorway. "Hey, what's up?" she asked.

"Hey yourself. I just heard that Lauren Brooks from the Sheriff's Office didn't show up for work the last two days. I guess she took Wednesday off but not Thursday or Friday. They think something might have happened to her."

"Lauren Brooks? Do I know her?"

"Probably. At least you must have seen her. She's one of the receptionists at the LEC. You know, where you pay your traffic tickets, or put money on someone's books over at the jail."

"Oh sure. I've met them both. She's the younger one, right?"

"Yeah. The older one's sort of an old hippie. Lauren's sweet. I took her to lunch one time; she helped me with a PowerPoint. She's friendly and like I said, helpful. Might have an actual work ethic."

"What do they think happened?"

"No idea, but I guess they did a wellness check on her house and found blood."

"God."

"I know." Diane tugged nervously at the scarf she wore. "Maybe she cut herself or something. Had to go to the hospital and was so injured she couldn't call work."

"That seems pretty unlikely," said Kayla, getting up and stepping into the hall. She noticed that other knots of people had formed. Diane and Kayla drifted into a nearby group. Everyone was talking about the missing woman. One of the men, a patrol officer she'd known for a short time, said, "That makes two missing women this month."

Kayla froze. Then she turned to Diane. "You know Bobby Jones, right?"

"Sure. nice guy—for a cop. What about him?"

"His wife is missing. She went to work and they found her car, but no sign of her."

Diane rubbed her arms as if she were suddenly cold. "You don't think they're connected?"

"I don't know, but I better tell someone about this. My boyfriend and Don Giggler have been sort of helping Bobby. Trying to figure out what happened, where she went."

"Well, surely the sheriff's office . . . "

"Of course. They're doing what they can but they thought—the guys thought—maybe it would be more effective to form their own think tank, try different directions. In any case Bobby had to do something."

"I guess that makes sense. I mean, I can't imagine what I'd do if my boyfriend disappeared. How do you even start to try and find someone?"

"Exactly."

"Especially if they don't want to be found," continued Diane.

"What do you mean?"

"What if she left because she wanted to get away from him? You hear about battered women, or psychologically tortured women running away. How do you know if this isn't a case of that?"

"First, I know Bobby Jones a little bit and I know how crazy he is about his wife. Second, why would she leave her car, her purse and pack nothing at all. No, it just doesn't add up . . ."

"I guess," agreed Diane, "Though if I was going to disappear I'd probably leave my car and my purse just to convince people like you that it wasn't my doing."

Kayla realized Diane hadn't really given up on her theory, so she simply nodded. Diane was subject to the very same flawed mindset that Kayla struggled with. When you worked in probation and parole sooner or later you started to believe that everyone was a bad guy—everyone was out to get you.

CHAPTER THIRTEEN

Wednesday, July 6, Afternoon

The day Chuck took Lauren was lovely and warm, with cloudless skies that reached across the valley and made a man feel bigger than his own skin.

He drove the van out to the woods where he'd parked the truck. It looked just as he'd left it, backed carefully into a side spur off a little-used logging road.

He parked the van and got out, hitting the button that automatically opened the side door, a feature he really liked. Reaching in, he unzipped the sleeping bag and flipped it open. He worked the bag off of Lauren's head, then untied the bandana and tugged the gag free. It had been clenched between her teeth. Unconscious as she was, he supposed it was lucky she hadn't swallowed it and choked to death. Maybe he didn't need it. They never made much noise once he hit them.

Soon after he freed her from the bag she came out of it, moaning to let him know she was still alive. He slapped her face lightly with his fingertips. There was a smear of dried blood across her lips and her skin was pale except for the pink mottling where he'd hit her before. Eventually the pink would darken to bruises. "Come on, wake up," he urged. He grabbed her shoulders and shook her. Finally she took a deep inhalation and groaned, then her eyes shot open wide.

Chuck grasped her shoulders to keep her from getting up but he needn't have bothered. She didn't struggle or try to rise. She seemed, despite her open eyes, to be asleep. He slapped her face again, harder this time. She reacted with an almost soundless moan, but did nothing else. Chuck pulled the rest of the sleeping bag aside. Her skirt had hiked up above her knees. He slid his hand up her leg from calf, to knee, to thigh. The skirt rose higher, gave him a glimpse of lacy pink panties. He licked his lips.

"What are you doing?" Bev asked, her timing, as usual, less than perfect. Did he dare continue? Would he be able to bear her wrath, her tongue?"

"Oh, shut up," he finally said, reasserting his role as the man in their relationship.

"You can't tell me to shut up."

"The hell I can't."

"You get your hands off that woman."

Chuck slid a finger inside the elastic band of the panties and tugged.

"Do what you said you'd do. Do what you promised," Bev shrieked.

"Shut up! Shut up! Shut up!" Chuck yelled, spit flying from his lips. He drew back his fist. When she didn't shut up he punched Lauren, his fist driving into her stomach. Again and again he struck out, hitting Lauren but wanting to hit Bev. Hit her, and shut her up for good.

When his arms were so tired he could barely lift them, he stopped. Gasping for air he looked down through the haze of sweat in his eyes. Wiping at them with the back of his hands he saw he was straddling Lauren's thighs. Her eyes were open but unfocused. She was still a pretty woman. His fists had fallen mostly on her body and avoided her face. He'd been afraid he'd see broken teeth, a smashed nose, or worse. It wouldn't have been the first time he let his temper get the best of him and that would be a shame. He'd learned a long time ago if he beat them ugly he was no longer interested.

"It's a good damn thing you didn't spoil this for me," Chuck snapped, but Bev seemed to have gone into hiding. That was the smartest thing she'd done all day.

Chuck again hooked his fingers into the waistband of Lauren's panties and this time pulled them off, tossing them aside. He wasn't going to waste a perfectly good opportunity. Unzipping his pants, he grabbed Lauren's ankles and spread her legs wide. She continued to do nothing but stare past him, at the ceiling of the van. It was disconcerting, but there didn't seem to be a thing he could do about it.

After a while he realized that something, maybe the excitement or the adrenaline—maybe the aftermath of his argument with Bev—was keeping him from finishing. He tried arranging her in a different way, rolling her onto her stomach and stuffing the sleeping bag under her hips to elevate them, then taking her from that position, but he found it equally unsatisfying. He was considering how else he might use her compliant, if not willing body, when he realized something was wrong. The shallow, trembling breaths she'd been taking had stopped. He reached for a pulse point on her throat. Nothing. She was dead.

"Damn it."

Thoroughly unsatisfied and full of rage he shoved her out of the van. Her body hit the ground, causing a puff of red dust to rise.

"Unbelievable. Just unbelievable." Frustrated, Chuck pulled on his pants and zipped up before climbing out of the van. Then he took a handful of Lauren's hair and dragged her toward the same ravine where he'd buried the other girl.

In the moonlight, the edge of the depression appeared like the jagged edge of a serrated knife outlined in silver. When he reached it, he dropped the body to the ground and then used his foot to push it over the edge. It slid into the waiting darkness of the ravine. His anger ebbed slowly as he went back to the van for a shovel.

"Chuck?"

"This is not a good time Beverly."

"I just wanted to say I'm sorry."

"Man's got needs, you know," replied Chuck tersely.

"I know, dear. I don't mean to be selfish. It's just so hard not to be jealous. Surely you understand that."

"I guess," he growled. Then, his voice grew softer, "No I do, I do understand, sweetheart." He looked for his leather gloves but couldn't find them. The van would need a thorough reorganization.

He took the shovel and began walking back, talking to Bev the entire time. "I know how hard this is on you," he told her. "It's hard on me too. You think I wanted to do that? What am I supposed to do with you gone? Only so much I can do with Rosie Palm and her sisters."

"My goodness, you're going to make me blush," Bev giggled.

"Yeah. You always were pretty old-fashioned about such things. Now don't go getting mad all over again. I always thought being old-fashioned was one of your charms."

"That's so sweet. Well, maybe the next one . . ."

Chuck stood at the edge of the ravine. "You mean you're okay with there being a next one?"

"Of course. We said justice must be served. Those men took me from you. It is only fair that you take their wives from them."

"And girlfriends," said Chuck. "Don't forget girlfriends."

143

"Is it that blue-eyed man's girlfriend you're thinking about?" Bev asked in a sing-song voice.

"Maybe," he said, teasing back. "She's a pretty little thing. Dark brown hair, sort of like yours, though not as long."

"You never did let me cut it."

"No I did not. A woman should look like a woman. But, honey, if it's going to make you feel this bad. I mean, if you really want me not to touch her before I kill her . . ."

"You are such a dear. That's all I wanted to hear. That you care about my feelings."

"Of course I care. I love you."

"Well, as long as I don't have to watch," said Bev reluctantly. Then, as a new thought came to her she said more firmly, *"Yes, you go ahead. That'll sure hurt those men, make them pay. Don't forget, you promised you'd get even with each and every one of them."*

"I did promise," Chuck said, "and you know I always keep my promises." Chuck tightened his grip on the shovel and headed carefully down the steep slope of the ravine. Under the inconstant moonlight that came and went behind fast-moving storm clouds, he slid down to what looked like a discarded pile of clothes. He hadn't had a chance for a cold kill and that was a shame but he'd do better next time.

His thoughts were already on his next target—blue-eye's woman—as he reached out and touched the body. It was warm and so soft, like silk under his hand, just like the poets said. Grasping an ankle he dragged the body the last few feet to the bottom of the hill. The scent of expensive perfume was out of place out here in the dust and pine, but it was still nice.

With no reason not to, and no one, not even Bev to stop him, he slid his hands into the dead woman's blouse, pulled her breasts loose of the confines of her bra and admired them with probing fingers. He slid his hands down her body and faltered a moment as he brushed the jagged edge of bone from a broken rib that had pushed through her skin. Ignoring that defect, he found her legs, those sweet shapely legs, and followed them to their apex where he discovered that she was still warm, soft and wet enough.

Bats flew through the trees, their wings trilling a soft back note as Chuck, grunting, drove himself into Lauren's body over and over until he finally found a satisfying release.

CHAPTER FOURTEEN

Tuesday, July 12, Evening

Kayla jumped sideways then caught at the rail to keep her balance.

"No, don't do that. Quit expecting yourself to fall. Let your weight come down on your toes and use your good foot to balance yourself. Trust your body. Come on. Do it again."

Kayla swallowed the argument on the tip of her tongue and jumped, this time to the left, landing on the edge of the silver duct tape Barb had placed there.

"That's it. Much better," Barb enthused.

Kayla wiped sweat off her forehead with the back of her hand. You are one evil trainer. That woman, what's her name, Jillian something? She's got nothing on you."

"Thanks. Just to prove you right, as soon as you're

done with two more sets of jumps we're moving into some agility drills. I'm gonna go set up some cones. When I'm done, you get to zigzag through them. I'll want you to move from one to the other, squat and touch each one. You're gonna love it."

Kayla groaned and jumped back into the middle of the box. Barb truly was a take-no-excuses trainer, and as much as she hated to admit it, just what she needed. She'd never been in better shape in her life and Barb was the reason. Barb, and not her own pitiful self-discipline, was the reason she'd been able to pass the search and rescue physical. She wished there was something she could do to repay her. Despite the rah rah attitude, Kayla sensed Barb was unhappy, her smile a mask hiding her true feelings.

Kayla finished the two sets of jumps, forward back and side to side. Her short, dark ponytail swung side to side as she moved. Finally she stopped to mop her face and neck with a towel and take a long drink from her water bottle.

As she caught her breath, she watched Barb winding back toward her, navigating between a row of treadmills that faced the long front window, and a row of free-weight benches along the back in front of a wall-length mirror. She was whistling, and when she dropped the final orange and white cone she grinned. To Kayla the grin seemed slightly demonic, or at least sadistic.

"Give a girl a minute to hydrate would you," she protested.

"So wise, using my own words back at me. Yes, hydration is important. You have one minute."

"Gah." Kayla took a sip of water then said, "You hear anything from Don about Bobby's wife?"

"Still missing, as far as I know." Barb ran her fingers through her short, wavy hair. It settled back in place as if it didn't dare not to. As usual, Kayla was struck by Barb's natural beauty. No makeup, wearing neon orange sneakers, black yoga pants and a slightly ratty white tank top she still managed to look wealthy and glamorous. No wonder half the women in town worried about letting their husbands get too close. Misplaced concern, thought Kayla, as she'd never seen Barb look at anyone the way she did at Don.

"Such a terrible thing to happen," Barb said. "Can't imagine what I'd do if Don just up and disappeared. Bobby must be insane with worry. Wish there was something I could do but as it is, well Don barely talks to me about it. Barely talks to me about anything." She said this with a shrug and a smile that quavered and then suddenly disappeared as tears unexpectedly filled her eyes.

Dropping to take a seat on one of the weight benches, Barb buried her head in her hands. "I'm so sorry," she said, her words slightly muffled, "I'm just having a bad day."

Kayla sat down next to the now sobbing woman, but did nothing while she cried it out. Barb wasn't the kind of person who would be comfortable with a hug or any acknowledgement. She would only be ashamed. So Kayla did nothing, and when the sobbing slowed, she walked to the front lobby, grabbed the box of Kleenex off the counter and returned with it. Barb pulled out several sheets, wiped her eyes and blew her nose.

"T-thanks," she said. "Sorry I lost it."

"I figure it was a long time coming."

"It was," Barb agreed.

"Don?"

"Afraid so. I just don't get it," she said, looking intently at Kayla as if she might hold the answer. "We don't talk. He works a lot of hours, and when he's home he's always busy working on some project or studying for some test. I suppose a lot of wives would think that's great. He pays the bills, mows the lawn, doesn't drink or do drugs or hell, even smoke cigarettes. God, sometimes I wish he would. You know, just be a total prick. It would be so much easier than this . . . this . . . I don't even know what this is."

"Back when we met everything seemed perfect, but after we got married things started to get weird, strained. The more he withdrew the more time I spent at the gym, working off the sex drive I guess," Barb joked. Her new smile, crooked and pain-filled was another failed attempt at pretending things weren't all that bad. Kayla wasn't buying any of it.

"Have you guys tried talking to a marriage counselor? Maybe he doesn't even understand that he's not spending enough time with you. Maybe this is how his parents were or something. If it's the only way he knows how to be . . . "

"I don't know. His mom died right before I met him. His dad's nice enough. Spends a lot of time out fishing with his buddies. We only see him on holidays and the occasional Sunday. He lives a good four-hour drive away, on the coast. You know how it is. We never seem to find the time to visit him. He doesn't want to make the drive. Too much effort. Anyway, I did ask Don about seeing a counselor once but he said it would look bad. He doesn't want to do anything that would slow down his chance of making detective."

"He's never made a secret of his ambitions."

"Yep. He's always chasing a goal. They say we marry our dads. I sure did. Don's so much like him. He was always driven and I saw how lonely my mom was. She kept busy with her groups and maybe it was enough. I'm not her though. I just don't like to drink that much." This time Barb's smile was genuine and Kayla smiled back. "Guess I'll just have to work harder to get the boy's attention. She shot a coy look over her shoulder and winked."

Kayla laughed, "I believe that might work. The way to a man's heart is, after all . . . "

"Through his penis? Yep, my momma taught me that much."

"I am shocked," Kayla declared.

"I doubt that," said Barb. "Now get off your rump and

get back to work. This little chat didn't fool me one bit. I know a distraction when I see one. Start at the first cone, bend and touch it. Keep up your speed by staying on the toe of your prosthetic foot and use your thigh muscles to extend your leg and your hip muscles as you turn or come up from the squatting position. Got it?"

"I got it. I got it." Kayla groaned as she moved to the starting position.

On the other side of town, while the sun disappeared like hope, fading into another empty night, Bobby Jones sat in his wife's favorite chair and stared at the television, tuned to a soccer game playing somewhere where it was bright and sunny and crowds cheered.

Around him lay his discarded uniform shirt, a tie, a half-empty bag of chips, and two Styrofoam boxes that had once held burgers, their sides slick with grease. He'd kicked off one shoe. It leaned against a leg of the entertainment center. On the small end table, the one he'd always hated because it was cute but almost too small to hold the remote, he had very carefully perched a half-empty bottle of pineapple-flavored vodka. How he had come to possess a bottle of pineapple-flavored vodka was something he'd deliberated on for a good long time.

Now he was moving on to other, more pressing concerns. For instance, why did he have a hole in his sock? Why did he take off the shoe that had covered the holey sock and not the other shoe which, he believed, covered a good sock wrapped around his foot? Though, on second thought, did a sock wrap around a foot, or was a foot inserted into a sock? It was an interesting thing to ponder. He wondered if Julie would have pondered this with him. Probably not. She was not one for pineapple-vodka or any kind of vodka for that matter. She liked a small shot of apricot brandy on particularly cold nights and that, as the saying goes, was that.

He remembered one crazy time when they'd gone sledding after an unexpected snowstorm. It was late at night, the neighbors were asleep and she'd woken him up, on a work night no less, and talked him into dragging her up and down the street on a sled. She promised she'd pay him back for the favor, and she had. They'd made love in the snow. Naked only where necessity demanded but still, pretty damn naked, and pretty damn cold, right there in the sort of hidden place between the wall of the garage and the fence. Two in the dang morning and crazy outdoor sex followed by a mad dash into the house, a hot shower and the taste of brandy on Julie's tongue as they'd slid into bed and made love again.

"Never that again," Bobby said to the darkening room, the only light the flickering TV screen, as the players swept across a field green enough to bring tears.

He took the bottle from its perch carefully and brought it to his lips. Pineapple when he'd been expecting apricot. Funny world, with Julie gone. And she was gone, he knew that for sure. He might not know a whole lot, but that, yeah, that had come to him today, easing into his stomach, stretching down his spine. Julie being gone was a hard fact that cut little bits out of him and left him hollow, sharp edged and fragile as old bone.

His chin nodded down and down toward his chest until he sat, like an ancient crone. One shoe on and one shoe off. Wasn't there some kind of poem about that? An old man who had a stinky shoe, whose wife didn't know what to do, so she put him in a pot and turned him into stew. That sucked.

He took another drink, a deep long swig that made him cough and gag and run, staggering into the bathroom, where he fell to his knees and threw up over and over. When he was done he slid to the floor, his face against the smooth, cool tiles. His tears were warm in comparison.

"He took you Jules. I don't know who or how or why but he took you and he killed you. It was too early. It wasn't fair. I'm gonna get him. Kill him good and forever. Break all his fingers for touching you. Break his legs for chasing you and his arms for holding you. I'm gonna snap his spine and then I'm gonna get mean. I'm gonna get him baby. Gonna get him," and on that promise, darkness came like a blessing and took Bobby Jones into a deep and fitful sleep.

CHAPTER FIFTEEN

Monday, July 18, Morning

Stenn and Kayla had agreed to meet Don and Bobby at the same Starbucks as last time. Stenn held the door and Kayla preceded him inside, where they placed their orders for house coffee. As hoped, their order arrived quickly and they joined their waiting friends.

A little over three weeks had passed since Julie's disappearance. With each day they had grown more desperate and less hopeful. As she took her seat, she noticed Bobby and Don looked drained and felt a pang of guilt for her recent happiness.

She'd spent the weekend in the Mount Hood Wilderness Area, training with NMR. She had acquired a rope burn on one wrist, a scratch from a thorn on her forearm and a raw spot on her stump from a stupid sock wrinkle. She wore these minor pains like badges of honor.

After a weekend of slogging down narrow trails slick with mud, climbing and repelling cliffs while sleet hammered down and sometimes sideways, she should have been exhausted. Instead she was elated. Though she'd passed her recertification weeks ago, it wasn't until the end of this hellish weekend that she'd come to believe she could do the job. With that realization, her mood had shifted, a sense of peace settling around her.

Or maybe the improved mood was just from spending time in the woods. There was always such a sense of calm there. She'd been raised in a home where the existence of God was a given and church was the center of community, but she'd never felt that sense of a presence greater than herself more than when she was outdoors.

As she took the same chair, in the same corner as last time, she realized Barb wasn't there. It was hard to ignore her absence, but she didn't want to ask Don where she was. After witnessing Barb's emotional breakdown at the gym, Kayla realized that as much as she'd like to believe she could stay neutral, she was a little uncomfortable around Don.

"I could have told you this on the phone I guess," Don said, "but I decided it would be better if we put our heads together. I have something to tell you, and a favor—a big favor—to ask."

"So get on with it," Bobby said, scratching at the stubble on his chin. "I've been waiting, but we're all here now, so what is it? It's about Julie, right?" The arrogance in his voice fell away on the last question.

Don's lips thinned in a grimace and he nodded, then, eyes locked on Bobby's he said, "The editor of the Observer received a letter yesterday from the person who might have taken her."

Bobby sat straight up in his seat. "What? Who?"

"I'm getting to that. Listen. Today, at the pre-shift meeting, we were told the editor of the Observer got a letter—actually a second letter—from someone claiming to have taken some women."

"Taken some women? What does that mean? What did it say, exactly?" Kayla asked.

Don shifted his attention to her. "It said, 'I've taken your women, just like you took mine,' and it was signed, An Angry Man."

"Are you sure?"

"I memorized it, word for word."

"I've taken your women?" Kayla repeated. "Women, not woman. Not just Julie. Do you think he's talking about Lauren? That's her name, right? The one who works the reception desk. Does he mean that he's taking women attached to the Sheriff's Office? Did he take Julie because she was . . . because she is married to a deputy, and Lauren because she works there?"

"That makes sense," said Stenn. "It's disturbing as hell, but yeah, sure. If those letters are real, then this guy is saying he's targeting the Sheriff's Office and going after women associated with it."

Don was shaking his head. "No, I don't think that's it. At least, I think it's not as broad as that."

Their puzzled expressions silently conveyed their confusion. All eyes were on Don.

He rubbed his hands together. "I'm trying to say I don't think it's the SO that's the target, I think it's us."

"Us." said Bobby.

"Us," Don repeated. "You and me, Bobby. I think it's *our* wives and girlfriends he's targeting."

"Why? Why would you think that?" Bobby asked.

"I was, hell, I was seeing her—seeing Lauren."

"But you're married," Kayla said, regretting the words as soon as they came out, as she realized how hopelessly naïve they made her sound.

Don glanced at her, then looked down, as if unable to meet her eyes. "I know," he said. "that's why I didn't ask Barb to join us. I don't want her to know about this. I don't want to hurt her. That's why I didn't say anything earlier. When Lauren came up missing so soon after Julie I kind of wondered, but I didn't have any proof and I didn't want to take the chance—"

"The chance? Take the chance!" Bobby exploded from his chair. It skittered across the glossy wood floor and smacked into the wall. Don started to rise, but too late. Bobby's fist was a blur as he punched Don in the face. Then he wrapped one large hand in the collar of Don's shirt and pushed him back into the couch cocked his arm back and hit him again and again, fast, accurate punches that landed with a wet, meaty sound Kayla would never forget.

Both Stenn and Kayla grabbed Bobby, tried to drag him off Don. He slipped from their grasp and hit Don in the chest, the shoulder, anywhere he could reach, but each swing grew wilder and less effective as they pulled him off balance.

Finally, Don managed to break Bobby's grasp of his collar and get free. They pushed Bobby face down on the couch and Stenn held his arms behind his back. "Settle down. Settle down," he said soothingly. Bobby's ribs rose and fell as he took huge breaths and huffed them out. Every muscle strained against their hold, Kayla's knee was firmly planted in his lower back, her weight resting on her forearms where she pressed against his shoulder blades. With a final shuddering breath, he stopped struggling.

Don had risen to his feet and moved around to the back of the couch, keeping it between him and Bobby. The two barista's stood behind the counter, eyes wide. The handful of customers sat frozen.

"It's okay," Kayla told them. "They're okay now." She didn't want anyone calling 911. That would be nothing but trouble and there was more than enough of that already.

"You gotta settle down," Stenn said to Bobby. "We need to hear what he has to tell us. What he knows might help us. You hear me?"

Bobby nodded. His face was still jammed into the seat cushions. Carefully Kayla and Stenn loosened their hold. He twisted until he was sitting on the couch facing them, his face red from exertion and anger.

"You done fighting?" Stenn asked.

"Done," he agreed.

"You?" Stenn asked Don. Don nodded. A thin stream of blood trickled from his nose joining the blood smeared around his mouth and throat.

Kayla went to the counter. "Thanks for not calling anyone," she told them gratefully. "You wouldn't happen to have a wet towel we could use?"

"Sure," said the girl, whose name tag read Alyssa. "We know you all are cops, so I guess it would be kinda strange to call the cops on you. You think those two are really done?"

"I promise," Kayla said. "They're friends usually. Just," she shrugged, "both having a bad day."

"I'd say," agreed Alyssa. She wet a towel in the sink, wrung it out and handed it to Kayla. Kayla carried it back to the couch and handed it to Don. He took it and walked around the couch, sat down and dabbed at his face.

"Better put your head back," Kayla told him. "Your

nose is bleeding."

He did so. In a moment, when he sat back up the bleeding had stopped. "Not broke," he told them.

"Too bad," said Bobby.

Don nodded, but said nothing.

"So, what does it mean?" asked Stenn, turning their attention from the fight back to the more important matter at hand. "Someone sent a letter to the editor. You say it was the second? What was in the first?"

"Same thing." said Don, holding the wet towel to his bottom lip, which was beginning to puff up. "Taking your women 'cause you took mine."

"And signed by an angry man," Kayla said.

"Yeah, every word capitalized. An Angry Man," said Don.

"What does he mean by 'you took mine'?" asked Don. "Is he saying we took his woman?"

"Maybe one of you arrested her," suggested Kayla. "Maybe she's in jail or prison? That might give someone a reason to hate you. Is there someone the two of you arrested when you worked together?" Kayla knew that Don had also been Bobby's training officer and had ridden with him for several months.

"That's a hell of a list," said Don.

"Really? Just how many women do you arrest?" asked Kayla.

"Yeah, I guess you're right," said Don. "We nail a hell of a lot more men, and of the women we do arrest, most of them get kicked pretty fast. There can't be that many. We need to go in and look at the records, do some research."

"No one else gets involved," said Bobby.

"What? Why not?" asked Kayla.

"You get the department on this it could screw things up, slow things down," Bobby explained. "It's our first lead."

"You're not thinking clearly," said Stenn.

"I'm thinking just fine, Bobby argued, his eyes hard in a way they'd never seen before. "You bring in the department and we have to do things by the book, maybe I never get Julie back. If that happens I'll hate you—all of you—forever. Never forgive you." His words, spoken in a near whisper, nevertheless resonated in the small space, powered by the strength of his conviction.

"They don't need us to tell them anything, said Kayla, "because we don't know anything that they don't. They already know about the letter and that two women connected to the department have disappeared. Knowing that Don was involved with one of them . . . I don't see how that would help."

"That's true," said Don, too eagerly.

Bobby shot him a look but then sighed and said, "Yeah, okay. I guess that's right. Forget what I said. My head's messed up is all."

Don looked at the floor between his feet, avoiding everyone's eyes. He didn't like being judged, especially when he knew he was wrong.

Stenn was right. He should have told them about himself and Lauren the minute she disappeared. Had he slowed up the investigation or was Kayla right and would the department already be looking at it the right way?

Having Bobby on his side, that was unexpected but he got it. Bobby wasn't worried about screwing up the investigation. He was worried that someone would get there first. For some reason, he'd decided that Julie was dead and he didn't want to see Julie's kidnapper locked up. He wanted to see him dead. Sitting there, his stomach churning with regret more painful than his smashed nose, Don vowed to make sure Bobby got the chance.

But there was something else he had to deal with right now. Barbara, and the pain it would inflict if she found out about Lauren. He had to protect her from that.

"I won't talk to anyone at the department," he told them. "I'll work it on my own and I'll find what you need, but you guys, you have to promise me you won't tell my wife about Lauren. I'm asking, not for me, but for her. I know you don't owe me anything and right now you might want to finish what Bobby started, but I'm begging you. Please don't tell Barb. I made a mistake, a really bad mistake. I won't make it again. I swear to you."

After a moment, Kayla said, "I can't speak for everyone, but I won't tell her. I don't want to see her hurt either. But you must promise to straighten up. Either be true to her, or leave her. No more chances."

"I promise," said Don.

"Okay," said Kayla, determined to leave it there.

"How about the rest of you?" Don asked.

Bobby nodded. "I don't give a damn who you sleep with. I just want my wife back. Whatever doesn't get in the way of that, I don't give a shit about."

Don looked at Stenn. "Okay," Stenn agreed. "Now let's get to work.

CHAPTER SIXTEEN

Monday, July 18, Afternoon

Chuck, sitting in his van outside Kayla's house, watched her drive up and get out of her Jeep. Her dark hair was tied back in a ponytail. She wore a fuzzy pink sweater, tight jeans, gray running shoes and carried a small purse with a long strap. The sweater looked soft and very touchable. So did she. The tip of Chuck's tongue slid across his dry lips.

A few moments later Stenn's truck pulled in, parked behind her Jeep and Chuck watched him get out and go inside. Chuck noticed that he didn't bother to knock, just walked in like he owned the place.

"Damn."

"What is it?" asked Bev.

"Blue eyes just showed up. That's not good. Besides,

her house isn't set up for this. Too open. Too many neighbors. Going to have to come up with something else."

"Well, I'm sure you'll figure it out. You're certainly smarter than they are."

A boyish smile crossed Chuck's normally impassive face. "Well, it doesn't take much."

After the fight with Bobby, Don went to the restroom to finish washing the blood off his face. He looked like hell and felt worse. His emotions were flip flopping between shame and a sense of dread. Not pleasant and not undeserved. Zipping his jacket up to his throat, to hide the blood stains on his shirt, he headed to work. He wasn't supposed to be there. It was his day off but if anyone asked he'd say he had to catch up on some paperwork. No one would question that.

Once seated in the small lint-gray cubicle he called his office, he dug out a bottle of ibuprofen and dry swallowed four of them. Bobby had gotten in a some good shots. His nose throbbed with each heartbeat, and an occasional sharp pain that felt like a spike being driven into his sinuses, made him wince. His left eye kept weeping too, making things blurry, which didn't help. He suspected that by morning the blotchy pink around his eyes would have turned dark and he'd have a couple black eyes to explain. No time to think about that or to pay attention to the pain though. He had work to do.

An Angry Man. Somewhere in his computer was the answer, a connection between him and Bobby, and some pissed off asshole. The problem was there were a lot of angry assholes; narrowing it down to one would be the tricky part. How long would someone wait to take revenge? Not long, he guessed. Not more than a year or two, maybe three. He set the search parameter to three years. Every incident report was scanned and archived. It took about a month, sometimes a bit more, depending on the number and staff capacity, before the reports were scanned and accessible digitally.

If the incident had happened recently he'd have to dig into the files to find the paper on it and, like most people, he hated searching through paper. With luck, he'd have ticked off An Angry Man sometime between six weeks and three years ago. "With luck," he said, barely breathing the words. Then he reached for his mouse and started to search.

After two hours Don knew that luck was not with him. He was tired and his head hurt from the combination of being punched in the nose and two hours of reading incident reports that were getting him nowhere. He wasn't ready to give up, but he needed a break and some fresh air. A quick walk around the building and a stop by the break room for some gut burning coffee should do it.

It was warm but the heat wave they'd been having was over. The sun on his shoulders felt good, and moving was doing what he'd hoped, waking him up. On his second loop around the building he went past the front door and turned at the corner where a group of lilac bushes hid the view of the brick and glass building. As he moved down the sidewalk past the lilacs he spied Lauren's coworker. She was standing on county property, clearly marked No Smoking, sucking on a plastic tube while streams of vapor wreathed her face. She didn't even bother to wear a guilty expression as he stopped, even though she clearly recognized him and knew he was a cop. He decided he liked the old lady, ink, dreadlocks and all.

"Any word?" he asked.

"Nothing," she said, not needing to ask what he meant. "You doing okay?"

He could tell she knew, maybe not all about him and Lauren, but enough. He decided not to try to play it off.

"No, I'm not okay. Not until we figure out where she is, uh . . .?"

"Martha."

"I should have known that."

"Yeah, you should have. But it's okay. I'll forgive you. I'm old and wise and shit." Taking a final lungful of vapor Martha slid the pipe into a narrow purse. "She the reason you're here on your day off?"

"Yes. I'm following a lead."

"What kind of lead?"

Don hesitated but then decided, what the hell. "Someone sent a letter to the paper saying he was taking our women. Signed it An Angry Man. Something about that is bugging me, reminding me of something. You know that feeling, like the answer is on the tip of your tongue?"

"Sure, I always say it's on the tip of my prefrontal cortex though. I think that's more accurate. But anyway, yeah I get it. So, how are you trying to track down this angry man?"

Don told her about his search, about the files he'd read.

"Did you look at the complaints?" she asked when he was through.

"The what?"

"The letters of complaint? The ones that get sent to the department from people pissed off by something or other. This angry man, he sounds like he could be one of those. You should look at those."

"You mean we have access?"

"Well, some of us do," Martha said, giving him a wide smile, showing off large square teeth. "You going back to the office?"

"Yes."

"Okay, I'll send you a link to the file. Give me about ten minutes. Gotta hit the little secretary's room first," she said, scrunching her face into a canvas of exaggerated wrinkles.

"Thanks," Don said, and meant it. The possibility of a new trail more than the short walk had brought him fully awake.

A few minutes after Don got back to his office, and only a couple minutes longer than the promised ten, his email signaled that a new message had arrived.

Martha Willow Weeping had sent him an email with the subject line, 'link.' When he opened it he found a link was the only contents. The link took him to a folder on the shared drive marked, as so many things were, with an acronym. This one read ECSOCF. He made a guess that it stood for Eulalona County Sheriff's Department Complaint File.

When he opened it he found pages ordered by year and date received. He scrolled back two years and began opening and reading files. He'd reached the fifteenth letter, scanned the salutation and signature, and felt a chill like the frozen fingers of a ghost was using his spine for a keyboard.

Sheriff
Eulalona County Sheriff's Department
233 First Street
Blue Spruce, Oregon 97332

Dear Sir,

On December 4 of this year my wife and I were heading home to Alaska from California where we'd been on vacation. I was driving my pickup and towing a 34-foot travel trailer. We were on Hwy. 97 just past the town of Blue Spruce and heading into the mountains. There was a steady snowfall, not exactly a blizzard but we definitely wanted to get through the pass before dark.

A row of semis was pulled to the side of the road and drivers were putting chains on. I believe one of these was blocking the chains required sign I was later told was there. I did not see the sign.

I was pulled over and the officer told me he would have to give me a ticket for ignoring the sign. I started to explain that the sign was hidden by the trucks but then decided why argue. I told him to go ahead and write the ticket. I was in a good mood and nothing was going to change it.

He then asked me why I was in a good mood and whether I'd been drinking. Dumbfounded, I told him that yes, I'd had two glasses of wine with an early lunch but that was several hours ago. He informed me that he would require me to take a breathalyzer. I said I would, though I was not happy about it.

It then turned out the breathalyzer didn't work. He called on his radio and a short time later another patrol car, this time with two officers, arrived. They did not have a breathalyzer but were asked to escort me back to the jail in Blue Spruce where the test could be administered. I was shocked and angry. I offered to do a field sobriety test but was told that because of the bad weather they wouldn't be able to judge it accurately.

The officers took me into town, leaving my wife stuck on the side of the road in below zero weather to keep an eye on our property. I was taken to the county jail and took a breathalyzer test there. When I was done I asked for a ride back to my vehicle but they said they were shorthanded and couldn't spare a car. They suggested I take a taxi which I did, at my own expense.

When I got to Alaska I contacted an attorney and found out that although I was not charged with a crime the DUI arrest is on my record. I am requesting, no demanding, that you expunge that arrest from my record. It is not fair and I want it fixed immediately.

With all sincerity,
Chuck Lewis, An Angry Man

Don remembered that day. He remembered with clarity as pure as the snow that had been falling, and he knew that Chuck Lewis was the angry man who had taken Julie and Lauren.

CHAPTER SEVENTEEN

July 20, Afternoon

Kayla had arranged to take Wednesday afternoon off because she had an appointment with her prosthetist, a word she hadn't even known before her accident. Dr. Hisikawa, or Dr. H as most of his patients called him, was small of stature but big of heart. He never failed to listen to what Kayla had to say, and remarkably, never seemed in a hurry to move on to the next in line. Both were traits which endeared him to Kayla.

"How's it been going?" he asked as he entered the exam room a moment after his soft rap on the door.

She smiled in answer to his wide, gap-toothed grin. "Been going fine."

"No swelling? No numbness?"

"No."

"Gain or lose any weight lately?"

"No, staying about the same."

"Good girl. Let's have a look." His assistant had already helped Kayla remove her artificial limb, liner and two socks. Dr. K leaned forward and took the stump in his steady hands. He rubbed and pressed various spots, then nodded. "You're right, things do look fine. You've done a remarkable job of adapting. Have you thought about what we talked about last time, getting fitted for a running blade? I know you volunteer with search and rescue and the extra springiness would certainly help with your energy expenditure."

Kayla said she'd consider it and took a brochure along with her. A running blade sounded great in theory but unlike her artificial foot it would look strange, robotic even. She couldn't wear it and pretend. Everyone who looked at her would immediately know that she was an amputee. Imagining the eyes of those strangers made her shudder. Once in the car she opened the glove compartment and stuffed the brochure inside—out of sight, out of mind.

Kayla's roommate had promised to make dinner for

everyone. Emma Jean was on summer break, and though she'd found a part-time job, she had more time on her hands than usual. Kayla was grateful.

"Something smells good," Stenn said when he arrived. He headed straight to the kitchen.

"Emma Jean made her famous baked mac and cheese with hot dogs, sprinkled with ranch flavored chips."

"The least healthy food groups you can find, mixed in one dish," Emma Jean bragged, as she pulled dinner from the oven. "Go. Sit."

"Don't have to ask us twice," said Stenn, "Just let me put this beer in the fridge. Anybody want one?"

"Do you all really need to ask?" said Kayla moving past him and sliding into her seat at the table.

Stenn smiled and pulled three longnecks free, holding them between his fingers while he put the carton in the refrigerator. Then he unscrewed their lids and handed them around.

"To good roommates," said Kayla holding her beer aloft.

"Who know how to cook," said Stenn.

"To cheese," said Emma Jean.

"To cheese!" they cheered.

Kayla and Stenn exchanged a glance. What would have been a somber dinner filled with talk of the missing women had been transformed. It would be good not to think about what was going on, at least for a little while. Emma Jean's dinner was a handy distraction.

Right after dinner, Emma Jean told them she was going out with friends and would be back late—very late. "No need to hang a sock on the door," she added with a wink.

"Thanks," said Kayla, winking back in an equally exaggerated manner. "I hate it when my socks get separated. So thank you for that too."

"Don't mention it," Emma Jean told her. "Stack the dishes and I'll do them when I get back."

Once she was gone, Kayla gathered the dishes and took them to the kitchen and Stenn got up to help. Kayla filled the sink with hot water and dish detergent. The smell of lemons filled the room.

"That's not stacking," Stenn said.

"Cook doesn't clean. At least, not in my house."

"Good to know," Stenn said, reaching for a dish towel.

"A man who helps in the kitchen. If I didn't know

better I'd think you were trying to get on my good side."

"Hmm," said Stenn, putting his arm around Kayla's waist and sliding it up and down. "I think all your sides are good."

Laughing, Kayla turned to Stenn and relaxed into him. The feel of his skin beneath the thin flannel shirt and the smell of his cologne were so familiar and comforting, she could shut off her thoughts and let her senses take over. His hands were slipping under her shirt, sliding across her skin.

He kissed her. He was a great kisser, his lips soft, his tongue hard and probing. Her fingertips slid into his waistband and he pressed his hips against hers in response. They came up for air, and then started again.

She felt his fingers on the front of her jeans, felt him twist the top button free, the slide of the zipper going down. Then his hand was in her pants, cupping her. This time it was her turn to press forward, grinding against his hand, sighing and gasping. He kissed her again; a deep kiss she moaned into.

Putting her arms around his neck she tugged him toward the bedroom. He ignored her and broke the kiss, then immediately moved his lips to her neck. She felt his mouth, his teeth nipping at the delicate skin there and she moaned again. Need was a wave that rolled through her stomach, a hunger that made her forget anything about shame.

Somehow, they found the bedroom and the bed. Somehow, they were naked when they reached it. The kitchen had been foreplay. The bed became an incredible tumble of their bodies, erratic rhythms that sped and slowed, sped and matched. Sweat slick, lungs gasping for air, sounds driven from between clenched teeth, first Kayla and then Stenn found what they needed.

"Damn, woman," Stenn said, his fingers wound in Kayla's hair, pulling her down toward his chest, from the perch where she'd ridden him to a damn fine finish. Then rolling to his side, taking her with him so they lay face to face. "That was . . ." He couldn't find just the right words. Instead he let her hair slide through his fingers, slid his palm over the curve of her waist, to the swell of her hips and then up along her thigh resting across his hips, to her knee, her calf. When his fingers touched the hard shell of her fake leg Kayla felt his body stiffen.

Her breathing quickened. She wanted to move away but fought the impulse. This was her body, her world, her reality. Any man who spent the night would see what was left of her—and what was missing. She bit her lip. She was being ridiculous. Stenn knew what had happened to her and he accepted her as she was. This was not the first night they'd been together. It was just the first time he'd touched . . . it.

She was relieved when he slid his hand back up her body and then rolled onto his back and stretched. She moved up to rest her head in the hollow of his shoulder.

"Mmm," he moaned. "Nice. You smell good."

"Lemon-scented dish soap," she said, then yawned, ready to slide into a nice nap.

"Sex, not soap. And don't start yawning. This party isn't over yet."

"Oh yeah?"

"Yeah, he said," and then unexpectedly he rolled over on top of her, pinned her wrists above her head and stared at her with such raw hunger it blew away every caution.

"Prove it," she whispered.

Later, after Stenn had fallen asleep, Kayla lay with her eyes wide open. This was it. Time to get ready for bed, and that meant removing the prosthetic. She never slept with it on. It was unhygienic and could lead to more sore spots like she got during her last outdoor training. But could she do that with Stenn right there in bed with her? He wanted her to. He'd made that clear, but he'd also sort of cringed when he touched it earlier. Should she wake him and ask him to leave? Was she ready for what she might see in his eyes when he looked at her, and saw that—that ugly word—her stump?

She was still trying to decide, when Stenn's cell phone began ringing. He started awake and immediately got up and started fumbling for his jeans on the floor. Kayla snapped on the bedside lamp and he stopped and looked at her sheepishly.

"It's okay," Kayla reassured him. "Get it. It might be something important, maybe your dad."

"Right." Stenn dragged his jeans off the floor onto the bed, dug his phone out of a back pocket and answered it.

"Lehrer," he said. Then, catching Kayla's eye he said, "What is it, Don?" pointedly letting her know who was calling.

"I'll be there in a few."

Thumbing the phone off he turned to Kayla and said,

"Don thinks he's figured out who the Angry Man is. I'm supposed to meet him at Bobby's. I'm sorry."

"Don't be. I'm going with you."

"That's great." There was a pause and Kayla saw him struggle for the right words. She knew he wanted to say something about spending the night. Knew he wished the phone call hadn't happened.

"We'd better get dressed and get over there, I guess," he finally said, putting off whatever he was going to say.

"You get the first shower."

"I'll make it quick," Stenn promised. He grabbed his clothes and moved toward the bathroom. He didn't invite her to join him and Kayla was grateful. She waited until the door closed before she found her robe, wrapped it snuggly around her and cinched the belt tight.

It was dark when they reached Bobby's house and the porch light was out, or off, but light blazed from the front window, open curtains allowing an unrestricted view of the interior. Even with the lights on it felt like a house that had been abandoned, thought Kayla. Shaking off the dismal thought, she rang the bell.

It was Don who met them at the door and invited

them in. They followed him to the dining room where they found Bobby sitting at a square table with four chairs, holding a mug of what looked like black coffee. He seemed to have trouble focusing on them with his red-rimmed eyes.

"Glad you're here," said Don.

"You said you think you know who the Angry Man is?" Stenn asked.

"Whoever he is, I'm gonna kill the son of a bitch," said Bobby, looking up blearily from his cup.

"Are you okay?" Kayla asked.

"Bob had a few too many," Don explained unnecessarily, "But he's working on that."

Bobby nodded vigorously, sending a small splash of coffee onto the table where it soaked into an open newspaper lying there. He stared at the dark gray blotch as if it were a puzzle.

Ignoring him, Stenn said to Don, "What do you know?"

"You told us about a letter someone sent to the paper," said Kayla. "You were going to follow up on that."

"I was, and I did. After you guys left I went to the office. Remember I told you I had a hunch about that angry man thing, that I thought that I'd heard it somewhere before? Well, I had, but I didn't find it right away. First, I got in and read a whole lot of old useless incident reports. But I didn't get anywhere. Then I—well I should say Martha found— Remember Martha? She's the woman that works with Lauren?"

Kayla appreciated Don's desire to give credit where it was due, but was impatient to hear what he'd found and only nodded curtly, encouraging him to continue.

"She got this idea," he continued, "that I should be looking at letters of complaint." He reached for a sheet of paper in front of Bobby that had just missed the spill, picked it up and placed it on the table in front of Kayla. "This is a copy of what we found. It's a letter signed, *An Angry Man.*"

Kayla spun the page a quarter turn so Stenn could read with her, bent across the page and began to read what turned out to be a letter addressed to her old boss, Sheriff Duncan.

"Go ahead and read it out loud," Don suggested.

She did, and when she was done she looked at the others. None of the three men would meet her eyes.

"I can see why he was mad," she said. I mean, getting

dragged to the jail because our equipment was faulty, that's one thing—but leaving his wife on the side of the road up in the mountains. That was just wrong."

No one said anything, and still, no one looked at her.

Understanding struck and Kayla said, "Don't tell me he's talking about you guys?"

Lips twisted into a grimace, Don nodded. "He was. We were helping the state police up at the chain up area just past the lake. You know what a bad spot that is. It was Stenn who pulled the guy over," He looked toward Stenn, as if sharing the blame might lift some of the weight of his own.

"He's right," said Stenn. "I remember that day. It was late afternoon, up on 97 along that stretch by Diamond Lake. Mostly I was trying to stay in everyone's mirror and get traffic slowed down. There was a bad storm coming through. I saw a truck and trailer fly past the chain up area, so I lit it up and pulled them over. The driver was . . . I don't know . . . funny. There was something off about him. Even before I asked him if he'd been drinking I thought, drunk or drugs maybe. His affect was off. You know how it is, right? Sometimes you get this gut feeling."

Kayla winced. Her phantom foot had decided that

was the right moment to send a piercing jolt of pain.

"You okay?" Stenn asked.

She shrugged off the question and said, "Go ahead. You were saying there was something off about him.

"Yes, but as I remember, it turned out he was clean, right?"

"Maybe," said Don. By the time we got him to the jail and tested, what with the bad roads and all, he would have been sober as a judge anyway."

"Chuck Lewis," Bobby spat, his voice loud and sudden.

Startled by his outburst, Kayla jumped but quickly recovered. "You need some more coffee," she said and took his mug, got up, ignoring the sporadic pains that shot up her leg, and went into the kitchen. It looked like someone, probably Don, had made some attempt at putting things in order. Dishes were drying on a towel on the counter and garbage had been stuffed into bags that sat in a corner, waiting to be taken out.

"Mind if I have some?" she asked, taking a couple mugs from a mug tree on the counter and carrying them to the coffee pot on the breakfast bar, which divided the kitchen from the dining room. .

"No. No, of course not," said Bobby.

The embarrassment he felt at his lack of hospitality was obvious. Kayla watched as he struggled to pull himself together, running his hand down the front of his rumpled t-shirt and then through his hair. "Anyone else want coffee?" he asked.

"I'm good," said Stenn.

"Sorry I don't have any snacks or anything. Julie . . . "

"It's okay," said Stenn. "We're not here for that. We just came to hear what Don had to tell us. Go ahead, Don."

"Okay, so yeah, Stenn pulled the guy over. Me and Bobby were riding together. I was his training officer back then. Maybe that's why I was being kind of a hard ass. That and the state cop was sort of an ass so I guess being a bigger ass was my way of impressing him."

"Well, at least you're willing to admit that," said Kayla, granting him what little grace she had to offer. "I do remember that winter. It was one of the worst winters we'd had in years. I had to dig my Jeep out every morning. It was miserable. I'm not going to forget it any time soon." She put a cup of coffee in front of Bobby but instead of returning to her seat she stood and leaned against the breakfast bar.

"Thanks," Bobby said.

Don continued, "So, Stenn pulls the guy over on a possible 12-31. I remember it was close to shift change so we were happy to provide transport. It was the last thing we had that day. As far as his wife goes, we offered to take her in with him, but he said no. Bobby even asked her if she needed anything. Help with the propane heater or anything. I mean—come on—we're talking about Bobby, right?"

Kayla looked at Bobby and knew it was true. He'd have never left someone in jeopardy. She liked to believe that none of them would have.

"Whether he had good reason or whether we were just doing our jobs, he was pissed off all right," said Don. "When we dropped him off he said it at least twice, 'I'm an angry man.'"

"And you think it's the same guy?" asked Kayla.

"Don't you? I mean, I didn't pay much attention when the guy said it when we picked him up. Lots of people are angry. But when I saw those letters to the paper were signed, An Angry Man, it kind of clicked. Maybe it's just coincidence but . . . "

"Yeah, but we don't like coincidences," said Stenn.

"No, we really don't," agreed Don.

Kayla said, "In the letters to the paper he say he's going to take your women. *Your* women. He means you guys, doesn't he? You are the *your*, and if that's true then we're your women, Julie, Lauren, me—oh—and Barb. Do you know where Barb is?" A surge of anxiety rolling through her.

"She's fine," Don reassured her. "She went to Taos to visit her folks. They live in a gated community, lots of gates and lots of security. I'm going to call her later and suggest she extend her trip."

"Are you going to tell her why?" Kayla asked. "I mean, don't you have an obligation to let her know she's in danger and what she should be looking out for?"

Don scrubbed his hands across his face and Kayla noticed how tired he looked, as tired as Bobby and even more disheveled. Evidence of the beating Bobby had given him was there. The skin under his eyes had turned a dark purple. She wasn't sure but thought she could see a rusty blood strain on the edge of his shirt collar. Kayla wondered about the marks she couldn't see, such as the destruction of their trust and probably their friendship.

"If I have to tell her, I will," Don was saying. "I just need some time. Need to see if we can get this figured out. If we can find him, find out what he's done with Julie and Lauren, then maybe she doesn't have to know everything. But yeah, when the time comes, I'll warn her."

Kayla nodded, took a sip of coffee, tried to imagine what Don was going through and failed.

"There's something else," he said. "After I got a name—"

"Chuck Lewis," said Bobby slowly, as if he savored the sound of it, trying out each syllable.

"Yeah, after I got his name I ran him through LEDS and Martha checked out the original arrest record, got the license plate on his truck. We ran it through DMV and came up with an address in Alaska."

Kayla's hand tightened around her coffee cup. For the first time in a long time she felt the stirrings of the hunt, that addictive sense of mission and a clear goal that no other work seemed to provide. "We have him." she said, elation bringing a lilt to her words.

He shook his head. "Afraid not. At least not yet. The truck he had, he sold about sixteen months ago, but we used the address to find out he'd also sold the house.

Before he sold there was a, oh hell I can't think of the name, should have asked Martha to sit in. Anyway, his wife must have died because there was something about her estate becoming his property. A bunch of legal jargon they use after someone dies. Probate maybe?"

"How did she die?" asked Kayla. Did it have something to do with them getting pulled over? Did something happen to her while she as waiting for him out there?

They all sat in silence for a moment, considering a woman stuck in a lonely trailer on the side of the highway surrounded by strangers, as a blizzard howled outside.

Don shook his head. "I don't see how. It wasn't like she was actually in the storm. She had a fancy RV to stay in. Plus, she wasn't out there that long. I mean, we cut him loose a couple hours later. He must have got back to his truck and went home fairly fast. Also, she didn't die right away. They were back home at least a couple months. I can't see anything he could blame us for."

"Okay," said Kayla. "I'd still like to know what she died from. She was in Alaska, but do you have the name of the town, the date she died? Maybe I can find a death certificate or an obituary, something that will tell us more."

"Good idea," said Stenn. "Anything we know is better than what we have right now."

Don nodded. "That's for sure. Martha's also working on something. When she was looking at the DMV records she found another car, a Camry, registered to the wife. There were two names on the title, the wife and someone with the same last name as her maiden name. We figure it's gotta be a relative, her mother maybe. Who else would you buy a car with?" She's trying to track that woman down. See what she knows. I think, if this is our guy—and my gut says it is—I think we're getting close."

Kayla took a sip of her bitter and now tepid coffee, made a face, but continued to hold the mug, unconsciously turning it in her hands.

"I don't know what happened on the side of the highway," Don repeated, "but whatever it was, I think he blames us. I figure what happened was his wife died, he blamed us, got rid of everything he owned and—"

"And came looking," said Stenn.

"And took Julie first," said Bobby. He placed the now empty cup of coffee carefully down on the table. "I told

Don I didn't want to call the office. Didn't want to share this with them. I wanted to find him first, you know." His eyes swept the room, stopping to make eye contact with each of them. When he looked at Kayla she nodded. Vengeance was not a concept foreign to her. She understood.

"No," said Stenn. "We share everything we know with the department. Everything." There was no ambiguity in his tone, nothing to make them doubt his words.

At that moment, Kayla realized Stenn was more cop than she was.

No one spoke. Kayla stood in the midst of the tense room, waiting for their response.

Finally, Bobby nodded, "Make the call."

CHAPTER EIGHTEEN

Wednesday, July 20, Night

Chuck parked his van a block from Kayla's house. It was o'dark hundred, navy speak for midnight, the perfect time to observe a target.

Clouds had scudded in to help, hiding the bloated face of the nearly full moon. Even the porch lights seemed to cooperate, pushing only feebly against the gathering dark.

The windows on both driver and passenger side of the van were down, letting in a warm breeze that carried the scent of melting asphalt, a reminder of the day's blazing heat. It had been unusually hot, even for mid-July, and he'd spent too much of it sitting in his van, nothing more than a metal box with upholstered seats. The tight pull of the skin on his left cheek and forearm told him he'd caught a bit too much sun. He'd develop a driver's tan, or in his case, a sit in the car and watch tan, if he kept it up.

"Too bad you don't have somewhere cold to sit, like a refrigerated truck," joked Bev.

Chuck fought the laughter that threatened to bubble from his throat. "Darn it Bev, I can't be losing it here. Cop might be sitting up at her house right now."

"Car's not there," Bev noted.

"Yeah, I see that. Don't mean they didn't come together, though they've never done that before, at least that I've been here to see. Think I'll risk it." Reaching into the cup holder in the van's center console, Chuck removed a small manila envelope. It held four valve stem covers that he'd picked up at a car parts store earlier in the day.

He took one out and set it open-side up on the dash. Then he put the envelope back, reached in his pocket and pulled out a small tube of super glue. He unscrewed the top, turned it over and used the pin embedded inside to poke a hole in the tube's protective foil cap. Despite the windows being down, the strong, acrid smell soon filled the van.

Taking the stem cover, Chuck squeezed a drop of glue inside and then set it back on the dash. Next, he scratched around in his pocket again, this time producing a BB trapped between two fingers. His hands had always been a little too big for truly delicate work. Frowning in concentration, he carefully brought the BB to the valve stem cover then dropped it inside onto the glue.

"Did it in one," he bragged to Bev.

"*I always said you could do anything you put your mind to.*"

"You sure did, honey."

"*Now what?*"

"Now we wait."

The persistent ringing of the phone dragged Kayla from a strange dream where she wandered through empty rooms in a house she remembered, but only from a previous dream. As she woke the dream disappeared like dust motes in shadow.

Opening her eyes just wide enough to make out the digital numbers on her clock, she saw the blurry red LEDs held a steady 3:11. Kayla groaned. Who the hell would call someone at three a.m.? It couldn't be good news. She fumbled for her phone on the bedside table, thumbing it on without bothering to disconnect the charger.

"Hello."

"Is this Ms. Fletcher, Ms. Kayla Fletcher," the caller asked. She didn't recognize the voice but there was a certain shaky timbre to it that made her think she was speaking to an older person.

"Yes?" said Kayla.

"This is Jack Holt at Melvin Morgan Memorial. Do you know a Stenn Lehrer?"

"Yes."

"He asked me to call. He wondered if you could meet him here, in the waiting room outside ICU."

"Is it his father?"

"I'm not allowed to discuss patients," the man said, "I'm just a volunteer making this call as a favor to a gentleman who asked."

Kayla was now positive that something had happened to Stenn's dad, another heart attack, one so serious Stenn didn't have the time to call her himself.

"Thank you," she said. "If you see him, please tell him I'll be there soon."

Fifteen minutes later she was sliding into the front

seat and starting her Jeep. The steering wheel was chilly and she shivered and blew on her cupped hands. According to the car's thermostat, the temperature had fallen to fifty-five from a high of ninety-five that afternoon. In the high desert the days could cook you and nights freeze you. She rubbed her arms, glad she'd slipped into a sweater but sorry she hadn't grabbed a jacket. Well, the heater would kick in soon. No sense running back inside.

Checking her mirrors and turning to look behind her, she reversed out of the driveway onto the empty street and then headed northeast. The fastest route to the hospital was the new bypass that skirted the edge of town. Though farther, it allowed for a lot more speed.

She had reached a straightaway and was moving from the posted fifty-five to a cautious sixty-five when she felt the car wobble. She fought the wheel and let her speed drop until she was practically crawling. Luckily the shoulder was wide and she could pull completely off the road. Two cars swept by in the far lane, their headlights sliding across her windshield as they sped in the opposite direction. She heard the hiss of their tires fading into the distance. Once that was gone the only sound was the peeping of frogs in the surrounding hay fields.

Hoping it would help other drivers see her on the dark road, she pressed the orange triangle on the steering column that would make her hazard lights blink on and off. Then she opened the door and stepped out onto the loose gravel and asphalt.

Sighing her frustration, Kayla moved to the back of the Jeep and looked down at the flat tire she knew she'd find there. Resigned to the task, she moved to the back of her car and unzipped the cover on the spare tire. She peeled it back then twisted the wing nut that held the tire in place. It was a full-sized tire and struggling with its weight, she lifted and pushed until it slid to the ground and bounced. She kept it from falling over and managed to lean it against the back fender. Next step was to find the jack.

She heard an approaching car slowing down and turned, shielding her eyes from the glare as it pulled onto the shoulder behind her Jeep. The headlights were blinding and she was grateful when they went off, leaving only the softer glow of orange fog lights. It was a van and she watched a man get out of it and move around to open the side door.

"Got my tools back here," she heard him say. Then he moved to the front of the van. Silhouetted in front of the fog lights Kayla noted that he walked slightly hunched, his steps slow and shuffling. An older man, she thought, from the era of rescuing damsels. "Looks like you could you use some help, young lady." Kayla gave him her biggest smile. She didn't want to seem unappreciative but she could change a tire by herself.

"Thank you," she told him. "It's just a flat and my spare's good. I should be fine."

"I'm sure you will be," he agreed. "You sure that spare's good?" He stepped past her and drove his knuckles into the top of the tire making the Jeep rock slightly. "Yep, seems fine,"

"It's not very old. I just had the tires rotated and—"

His arm moved in a blur and there was pain, sudden blinding pain that sent tracers across her vision and took her strength. She would have dropped to her knees but strong arms caught and held her.

From the periphery of her vision a dark stain grew. When she blinked, it receded slightly. Trying to raise her hand to her head she found her arms were pinned to her sides. She felt her toes skid across the ground and realized she was being dragged. Then she was falling and tensed automatically but instead of hitting the ground she fell onto something soft. Her hands free, she immediately reached for her head, cradling it between her palms, trying to stop the throbbing pain.

Her fingers found a bump above her left eyebrow and she winced then probed the sore spot. The bump was growing bigger, but there didn't seem to be any blood or broken skin. She wasn't sure what had happened but at least she knew her body was intact. The reassurance helped push away the dizziness and fuzzy thinking. She became aware that she was lying in the back of a van and that the old man was pushing at her trying to get her farther into the van. She rolled toward him fast, aiming her elbow at his chest.

The slap of his fist against her left ear sparked a fresh torrent of pain that tore her breath away and made her eyes water so much she couldn't see. She punched at him but her blows were weak and he batted her away as if she were a kitten. He shoved her face against something soft, like a blanket, but when he started zipping it up she realized it was a sleeping bag. The darkness and the closeness of the bag drove her into a frenzy. She kicked and punched and squirmed, fighting to keep the bag open, fighting to reach light and air.

He dug his knuckles into her thigh and instinctively she moved away from the pain. This allowed him to finish drawing the zipper the rest of the way. She screamed a scream so loud and long it tore her throat and she coughed. She couldn't breathe. The sleeping bag seemed too thick to let in air. She was panicking, knew she was smothering. She twisted, turning her face to the side, pushed her hands against the bag so that it formed a small space where her face was free of the constricting cloth, where she could breathe again, think again and fight the swell of panic that being locked in threatened to reignite.

Taking slow, calming breaths she told herself this was not the time to lose it. She had never been claustrophobic and she'd been tested plenty of times.

She'd started exploring caves when she was twelve, slowly graduating from amateur spelunker to caver. Her parents had taken her to Tulelake, California to visit Captain Jack's and the Lava Beds National Monument at least a couple times every summer. They were the caves where a handful of Modoc Indians had held off hundreds of soldiers and made themselves legends of tenacity and bravery.

Growing up she'd caved every chance she could, had joined a club in college and had never been afraid to test the boundaries. In fact, in the club she was known as the one they sent in first because of her willingness to belly crawl through the narrowest tubes, hands stretched far in front as if she were swimming, holding her breath so she could squirm forward another inch. She'd been lucky, only getting stuck twice. Both times she'd stopped, counted to thirty to calm her breathing then worked her way out leaving more than a little skin behind. Calm reason and not panic was the only way out. This situation was no different.

Think.

He had her, the same guy who had taken Julie and Lauren had taken her. This was no coincidence. The idea that this was some random kidnapping wasn't worth wasting her time on. The more important question was; where was he taking her and what was he going to do when they got there? Julie had been gone for weeks. Was she alive? Locked up somewhere? What about Lauren? Were they both dead? Was that to be her fate as well?

No, she couldn't go there. She had to reason her way out of this.

Think.

She was zipped in a mummy bag with her feet where her head should be. The top of the bag was tied shut and there was no way for her to turn around in the confined space. But maybe, just maybe there was enough wiggle room . . .

Rolling to here left side, Kayla reached into her back pocket and felt the reassuring shape of her knife. It wasn't anything fancy, just a three-inch blade that folded away. A tool for cutting rope, or tape, or removing the price tag from a last-minute gift she'd bought and had to wrap in the car.

She brought it to the front of her body slowly, and grasped it with both hands. The uncomplicated wood and metal was reassuringly familiar. She felt for the blade and worked it open. Every instinct demanded she stab the blade through the suffocating fabric and tear it away. Only iron determination and caution stopped her. Cutting the fabric would make a noise and get his attention. The last thing she wanted. She'd wait. When the van was moving—when there was road noise—that was the right time.

She rolled onto her stomach. Her body would help to insulate the sound of ripping fabric. She carefully slid the point of the knife into the thin material, pushed past the batting and through the other side. The small victory, and a whiff of fresher air gave her renewed hope. Now she just needed patience.

The van made a tight left. She had to fight against centrifugal force trying to roll her onto her side. The noise of the tires seemed quieter than she'd hoped. She'd have to go slowly.

A few minutes later the van took another turn. She remembered when she went into the bag she'd been on her stomach and the door had been on her right. Now, on her back, the door must be on her left. Or so she thought. Nothing seemed certain, except that getting through that door was her only chance.

She'd have to be ready. Once he saw she was free he'd probably slam on the brakes. When he did, she'd move fast, maybe call him by name, shake him up. Don had said his name was Chuck. That might surprise him enough that she could get away, then it would be just a manner of running. Running was easy. Well, it had been easy before the shooting, and she'd been practicing, getting better. This guy, this Chuck, was old.

Even as she tried to convince herself, she could remember the way his arms had wrapped around her, strong arms that had carried her to the van and held her down almost effortlessly. He might be old, but it wouldn't be smart to underestimate him.

The van slowed, and Kayla braced as it took another turn, this time to the right, and in a few moments, another left. Given all the turns, Kayla decided that Chuck must have decided to go through town and had been weaving through the downtown corridor. Realizing that the sound she'd begun to hear through the muffling effect of the sleeping bag was traffic Kayla guessed they'd reached the highway. The sound of big rigs rolling by was terrifying. It meant they were heading away from town, away from Stenn and any sort of help. It also meant she could risk making more noise.

Grabbing a handful of fabric, she held it taut. This time the knife sliced through several inches. She could reach through the gap, if she dared. But she didn't dare. If he saw her arm he'd stop and come back and maybe hit her again. Hit her more than once.

Panic began to overwhelm her, turning her from a thinking creature to something of blood and bone and instinct. She had to keep her head. She was alone out here. That last turn had been long and slow, an on ramp. Had he turned right or left that time. She couldn't remember. The throbbing above her left eye had become a continuous ache. She brought a hand up; her cool fingers were soothing. Blinking, she realized how dark it was. She could only make out the barest shadow of her eyelashes and the dark on dark line of a seam inside the bag. The air seemed to hold too little oxygen and she wondered if her thinking had been affected.

What had she learned in high school from Mr. Faulk, her biology teacher? People breathe in oxygen and breathe out carbon dioxide. Is that how it works? What would happen if you had too much carbon dioxide? She wished she'd paid more attention. It was a stupid thing to worry about anyway, there was a huge hole in the bag now and plenty of air was flowing in.

A trickle of sweat ran down the side of her face. Or was it a tear? She wasn't sure.

After what seemed an eternity she managed to slit the bag open several more inches. Bits of batting sprung out, a white froth. She hoped none had escaped to give her away. All she had to do was reach out, grab the door handle and jump free.

The problem was, the van had picked up speed and she was sure if she jumped out at that speed the impact would kill her. But if it slowed down, that's when she'd be all in.

Liar. Just do it!

Almost as she thought it, the van slowed and there was a jarring bump. Kayla grasped the knife.

Had they turned off the highway? She pushed her head through the slit in the bag, struggled to get her shoulders free, reached for the door handle and pulled. The door was locked. Panting like a cat she felt for the lock, disengaged it and the door began to slide open. She pushed it open wide, saw the ground rolling slowly by, as slow as walking, and pushed herself through feet first.

Instead of feeling her feet hit the ground, she was jerked backward into the van.

Chuck had seen her emerge from the bag and quicker than thought had yanked the wheel and driven onto the shoulder. He'd barely had time to pull over—the van was still in gear, rolling slowly forward, but he ignored it and threw himself between the seats, grabbed the bag and jerked her back into the van.

"You sonofabitch!" she screamed and lunged toward him. He felt the knife go into his bicep. It hurt like a mother and he swatted her backhand. The knife flew across the cab and landed on the seat with a dull thud.

The van lurched, front tires bumping over something, and came to a stop.

He grabbed her arm and she tried to pull free, slapping at him, scratching with her free hand. He couldn't afford to lose her, not here on the highway, out in the open.

"Let me go," she said. Let me go—Chuck."

The sound of his name startled him. How did she know . . . ?

Breaking free she dove for the open doorway.

"Damn it,"

She was out. She was running.

Chuck went after her, but she was fast and he was torn between chasing her and getting the hell out of there.

Then, for no reason he could see, she fell, landing on her hands and knees. Without slowing he reached her and slammed his fist into the back of her head. She sagged to the ground. A couple of cars went by, their tires whining as they sped along. He froze but they didn't slow, the van blocked their view of her. Grinning at his luck, he reached for her ankle, planning to drag her back to the van.

The blow that drove her to the ground set off sparks behind her eyes. She fought free of the daze in time to feel his hand on her leg, to feel his eyes, as unwelcome as his touch, on her body. She shivered. Weakly she tried to move away but only managed to roll to her side, propped up enough so she could see him looking at her. Suddenly she felt the pull of her prosthetic where it cradled her leg.

"What the hell?" he exclaimed and yanked his hand away as if he'd been burned.

Kayla drew her "bad" foot back and kicked with all her strength. The jolt of her foot meeting his face resonated all the way to her hip.

The impact knocked him backward, his arms pinwheeling as he tried to keep his balance. Even before he hit the ground Kayla was moving. No time to decide where she should run. She just ran.

The sun, rising through the distant trees showed a narrow deer path into the forest. She almost hesitated. Shouldn't she stay on the highway and flag someone down? But the risk of him catching her before she could get someone's attention on this stretch of road so far between towns was high. The van was still running. On the highway he could run her down easily. In the trees she might be able to elude him.

She plunged down the trail and into what she hoped was the shadowy safety of the forest.

The narrow path took her to an old logging road with two overgrown lanes running perpendicular to the deer trail and parallel to the highway. She turned right, in the direction she thought town was, and moved into a jog, glad for the smoother surface.

As the pounding of her heart slowed she began to hear an ominous creaking. Around her on both sides of the road the weak light painted the edge of trunks and branches gray. An unusually wet fall followed by a winter of heavy snowfall had caused many of the trees to snap near the ground. Some were kept from falling by the branches of neighboring trees, but the lightest breeze filled the woods with the rasp and groan of wood against wood, and the constant weight made branches snap with a sudden sharp crack. The sounds made her anxious, afraid she couldn't hear him coming, but it would mask her footfalls as well.

She had no plan, just instinct. It told her to run and hide. She'd been running, but now, straight ahead, a line of red-limbed brush brought her attention to a rock wall at the base of a hill. The wall rose well above her head, maybe sixteen feet she estimated. It was crowned by densely packed pines and more of the same brush.

The road curved around the small hill to the right. The road was the easier path. He'd probably think she'd follow it. Instead she turned left at the wall, away from the road. The ground sloped downward and she slowed, taking careful steps as it became steeper with exposed rock threatening to trip her.

A break in the wall formed by a landslide looked manageable. Rain or melting snow had carved a path through the young brush. If she could climb to the top, then follow the ridge to the top of the rock wall, she'd have the high ground, maybe see where he was and what he was doing.

With luck he'd already given up. If that was true all she had to do was climb back down, get to the highway and flag down a ride. Her adrenaline-fueled imagination played scenarios of getting to the highway, thumbing a ride and out of nowhere seeing a white van barreling down at her, a grinning Chuck Lewis at the wheel. Or maybe getting in the car of a stranger, only to find he was Chuck's accomplice. She knew these scenes came right from the pages of the horror novels she liked to read. It didn't make them any less real.

She shook them off. Eventually she'd have to get to the highway, get to town and go right to the Sheriff's Office where she'd tell them everything she knew. No more playing detective. She'd tell them she was sure the man who had taken her was Chuck Lewis. As she'd hoped, he'd been surprised at the use of his name. That was enough for her. Don had been right and that meant he had probably taken Julie and Lauren the same way. What had he done to them after he took them out of the sleeping bag?

A shudder ran through her. Wanting to hurry, she forced herself to move slowly, carefully. She was not at her best.

In the distance, she caught the hiss of tires rolling on asphalt. It was the sound of cars rushing by on the highway that seemed so close and yet impossibly far away.

An engine roar suddenly filled the air, echoed from the hillsides. Kayla dropped to a crouch. Light swept across the hillside. The van was coming, bucking down the logging road, heading straight toward her.

CHAPTER NINETEEN

Thursday, July 21, Morning

Don stood, shoulders back, stomach tight, transported back to his time in the army, where he'd put in his four years, except for basic training, as an MP in Germany. Going from military police to civilian police had been step one in a plan he'd concocted his senior year. Something to get him far away from home. Never thought the first job offer would come from the hometown. Fate was a bitch.

"We do not go off and run investigations," Sergeant O'Neil said in a tone strident enough to keep Don's attention. "We trust the men and women we work with to get the job done. What you have done by forming this special group is to alienate your coworkers and interfere with an investigation. Do you hear me?"

"Yes, Sir," Don replied. There was nothing more he could say. He'd explained that they'd only wanted to help Bobby Jones find his missing wife. That they had planned to share everything with the department, but there hadn't been much to share. He half suspected that O'Neil wasn't so pissed about the off-the-clock investigation as he was about its lack of success. He could understand that.

O'Neill raked his fingers through his graying brown hair, then smoothed what some of the guys jokingly called his porn 'stache.

"We don't get into fist fights in coffee shops either," O'Neil continued. "The public expects more from us. They *should* expect more from us. Isn't that right, Don?"

Don's spine loosened a fraction at the use of his first name, though his abused stomach continued to churn.

"Yes, Sir."

"Good. Now look. I can appreciate how much you guys want to help Bobby, but with the disappearance of Lauren Brooks and the suspicion that the two are related we're moving this from a missing person to a possible kidnapping. The FBI office in Portland has been contacted. We don't want to mess this up," O'Neill told him. He didn't have to say we don't want to mess this up in front of the feds, but Don understood perfectly.

"No, Sir."

"So, what do you do next?" O'Neil asked.

"We've shared everything we know. Right now, we're waiting for our suspect's sister-in-law to arrive. When she does, we'll bring her to the office for questioning. Hopefully she'll be able to tell us something useful about him."

"We can only hope," agreed O'Neil. "Now get out of my office."

Don nodded and did as he was told. He knew how thin the ice was under his feet.

He'd told the sergeant everything he knew about the disappearance of Julie and Lauren, about the angry man and their suspicions. He'd told them the angry man was probably Chuck Lewis, but he hadn't said a word about having a relationship with Lauren. That would be career suicide. Not that he'd had an affair, but that he'd failed to mention it once she went missing. It was a possible link, a part of the puzzle, and he was withholding it.

He'd let O'Neill believe it was working at the SO's

office that the group believed put her in Angry Man's sights. He knew Bobby and the rest of them hadn't been too happy to help him cover his ass. Part of his argument had been that such a little detail was unimportant in the scheme of things. Now all he had to do to prove it was solve the case before anyone else.

The only light at the end of that particular tunnel was Jessica Locklear, sister of Beverly Lewis, wife of Chuck.

It hadn't taken Martha long to find the woman listed as co-owner of Beverly Lewis' Camry. Don hadn't wasted any time in calling her at her home in San Francisco.

Jessica Locklear was omission number two, because though Don had told his boss about her, he'd failed to mention that she'd changed her original travel plans and would be arriving, not on Wednesday night, but this very morning.

It had been a lucky break. Don wanted to talk to her first. Maybe what she told him would be key. He had to be the one to find Julie and Lauren and catch the bad guy. It was the only way he could think of that would keep Bobby Jones from destroying his career, or maybe taking a shot at him from some dark alley some night, and the sad truth was, he wasn't sure he would blame him if he did.

The plane landed late, but just in time. Another moment and Don would have thrown something through the wall-length window overlooking the tarmac. But the plane did land, and he watched eagerly as the dozen or so passengers left the bright blue and yellow craft and descended the staircase.

He spotted her right away. It wasn't hard. Most of the passengers traveled in pairs or groups and the only singles were business people wearing suits and lugging carry-ons and laptops. Only one middle-aged woman marched across the shimmering asphalt and entered the lobby alone. He crossed the small space in three long strides. "Ms. Locklear?"

"Officer Giggler." She put out her hand and gave him a no-nonsense handshake while giving him a look of frank assessment. There were wrinkles around her eyes and bracketing her mouth, and her hair was gray, a thick mop of wavy curls held back by a pair of bright pink reading glasses perched on her head. But despite these signs of age, she dressed like a younger person, a black knit shirt with long sleeves, faded jeans and black dingo boots. When she headed toward the luggage carousel Don noticed she didn't move like an older person either. She was reaching for a small black bag and he reached past her and took it.

"Let me get that for you."

For a moment her light gray eyes seemed to darken but then she nodded curtly. "Please."

"Did you find a hotel?" He asked, trying to get beyond whatever mistake he'd just made.

"Yes. Eagle Ridge. I understand there's a small restaurant. I thought we could talk there. I have some things to show you. She tapped her fingers on the huge leather purse slung over her shoulder. We can talk on the way though."

Don nodded.

In Don's car, heading toward the Eagle Ridge Hotel she said, "Your phone call was a surprise."

"I was hoping you'd know where your brother-in-law had moved after your sister . . . "

"You can say it. You can say after she died. But please, don't call him my brother-in-law; let's just call him Mr. Lewis."

"Of course," he agreed. "You know, you didn't have to fly all the way here. Whatever you had to tell me you could have told me on the phone."

"No, I couldn't. I really couldn't. It's too . . . well it's weird. Too easy to dismiss as just some crazy woman's crazy ideas. I need to lay it all out. Show you the evidence I've collected. Then you can judge. For now though, can you tell me more about what's happened here? I understand a woman is missing, and you presume that Mr. Lewis is involved."

"That's right." Don filled her in on the disappearances of both Julie and Lauren, again omitting his relationship with her. By the time he finished telling her the rest, they'd arrived at her hotel.

The restaurant at the Eagle Ridge hotel was decorated with a rustic western theme. Walls were natural pine, and booths were divided by low partitions of river rock. A small gift shop at the front sported items for the tourists: cowboy hats; stuffed toy owls, elk and bear; and plastic fish mounted on plaques. At the entrance to the restaurant a sign invited them to seat themselves.

Don took the lead and found them a booth in the back. After slipping to the center of the red faux leather seat, she pushed the wire cage of jelly selections and a sign advertising the day's dessert choices to the side, pulled a file folder from her purse, and laid it in the center of the table. She placed her palm flat against it, holding it against the table as if she didn't trust gravity to keep it there. Then she looked up into Don's eyes and said, "The worst of it is, I knew. I knew it all along." She paused and Don saw that despite her brisk, no nonsense act, her lower lip was trembling slightly and her eyes were glossy with gathering tears.

"What did you know?" he asked. He almost reached across the table to touch her arm, to offer comfort, but he didn't know her well enough.

"I knew that eventually that son of a bitch would kill my sister. I knew it like I know the sun will set. But I could no sooner explain why than I could explain astronomy.

"No, damn it, that's a lie" She swiped at an errant tear that had slid down her cheek. "I guess I wanted to believe his lies almost as much as she did. My sister was lonely most of her life. She was pretty enough and smart, but everything was so serious for her, so intense. I think it scared a lot of the guys off. She wasn't very good at playing the dating game. I'm not sure she realized there was one. She had a serious relationship for a time. They even ran off to Reno and got married. It was one of those college things, sort of a lark. He left her before their first anniversary for someone he told her was more exciting.

"She was devastated, buried herself in her studies, got a degree in history and then in education. Instead of teaching, she did two years in the Peace Corp. Then she seemed to settle down and for a few years worked for a private school in Simi Valley, California. She told me it wasn't horrible but she felt invisible there, not essential and easily replaced; do you understand?"

"I do. I'm sure most of us feel that way."

"Yes, but for her, with no one special in her life . . . I think it was harder for her because her job was all she had. It meant more to her than it does to people with families, with kids. She had to keep looking for the right place, the right job. She heard about a teaching position in Alaska and she took it."

The waitress appeared and they scrambled to look at the menu. As soon as the waitress left with their order for stuffed hash browns and coffee, Don asked, "So, did she find what she was looking for in Alaska?"

"She did. She got to work with Native kids. She loved it. She loved them. The classes were small, so she got to know them in a way she couldn't know the kids in California. Those were connections. She was happy." Another tear slid down her cheek. This time she tugged a paper napkin from the dispenser on the table and patted it away while giving Don a crooked smile. "I'm not usually such a cry baby. I've worked for the San Francisco District Attorney's office for nearly thirty years. I've heard stories that are cry worthy almost every day."

"But this is your family," said Don.

"I guess."

The waitress brought ice water and poured coffee. Ms. Locklear tore open several packets of creamer and poured them into her cup, then added a packet of sweetener. Having something to do seemed to help calm her. She sipped at her coffee while Don fished an ice cube from his water glass to drop into his steaming cup.

"Beverly loved Alaska all right. I think she really loved the not-California of it. The culture was different, the weather was different. I think she especially liked proving she could handle the cold, the slippery roads, the winters when so many people fled to the lower forty-eight. I think she would have been okay, but then she met Chuck."

"He told her he was retired from a career with the military, the Navy, and that he moved to Alaska because it was the one state he'd never seen. I think he liked the wildness of it. The chance to maybe be free of some of the rules. But I don't know Alaska that well and maybe I'm painting a picture that isn't true. Anyway, he liked to hunt and fish but he told her that got sort of boring and he decided to go back to working. He took a job driving a delivery truck. One of his routes was delivering food to her school."

"He'd come in after unloading and have a cup of coffee in the teacher's lounge before heading back out. That's how they met. At first I was happy for her because she seemed so happy. I hoped it would last. That they'd date for a while and then he'd move in or she'd move in with him and maybe in a year or two they'd marry. But it didn't play out that way. It moved way faster. First, she tells me she is seeing someone. Barely six weeks later they're engaged, and then maybe two weeks after that she sends me a card inviting me to her wedding, along with a note saying it was just a sort of courtesy because she knew I couldn't get away on such short notice. I checked the invitation and sure enough, the date was in two days! None of the family made it to the wedding. There aren't many of us, our parents died when we were in our twenties, but there are two aunts, an uncle, and a cousin we grew up with. You'd think she'd have wanted some of us there. "Maybe it sounds like we weren't close but—"

"But you were sisters," supplied Don.

"Exactly. We were sisters and to not invite me . . . In my career I've seen more than my share of abusers and cutting someone off from their family, that's one of the signs. Why I didn't see it . . ."

"It's harder when it's your own family, Ms. Locklear."

"Call me Jess, please."

A different waitress arrived and put their plates in front of them, refilled their coffee cups, complimented Jess on her leather bag and shot Don a wide smile before walking away, her hips swaying.

"Working for that tip?" suggested Don. Then wished he could take back his inappropriate remark.

"Or she's actually attracted to you and figures being nice to your mother can't hurt."

Relieved, Don realized he liked her.

There was a short pause in their conversation as each fixed their coffee the way they wanted and took a few bites of breakfast.

"Yours okay?" Don asked.

"Bacon's a little salty," said Jess, dragging her fork through the potatoes. "They take your salt away when you get old, then all you taste when you go out is salt."

Again, Don felt the little buzz of affection. "So, you went to Alaska. How did that go?" he asked, taking the conversation back to where they'd left off.

"It went fine. Great in fact. They were so perfect and so sweet to each other it made my teeth ache. I was expecting some bossy guy, you know, lifer military, all rules and regulations and my way or the highway."

"He was nothing of the sort. Well, he was very orderly, very organized but able to fit himself around her. Remember, my sister had lived alone a long time by then. She had set routines that used to drive me crazy, but he didn't seem to mind. He cleaned up after himself and spent a lot of his spare time in the shop he built behind her house making things for her. She told me when she wanted something repaired he repaired it. He was like the dream guy who prioritizes the stuff on the honey do list over his own stuff. She bragged about it, of course, what woman wouldn't?"

"She really did seem happy. After the two weeks were over I decided I'd made a mistake and went home."

"And then?" Don asked.

She didn't answer right away. Instead she pushed her nearly full plate away and took another sip of her coffee. Then she set the mug down but kept her hands wrapped around it.

"And then I started having problems reaching her. It wasn't like we talked every day, but I did try to call at least once a month, you know just to check in. Alaska is a hell of a long way from San Francisco. I worried about her out there in the middle of nowhere. She taught in the village where she lived, but sometimes she'd get called in to sub for someone that was way out there, and she'd fly in some little rickety looking plane. She was even taken on the back of a snowmobile a couple of times. I was waiting to hear she'd gone via dog sled eventually." Jess smiled at the memory, the wrinkles around her eyes crinkling. Then the smile disappeared.

"I'd call and no one would answer. When she'd finally pick up she'd say they'd been having trouble with the phones, reception was bad, whatever. Never had any trouble before Chuck moved in. Of course, back then I didn't even think to question it. Now, as I'm looking back, I'm questioning everything."

She picked up one of the empty sweetener packets and began to fold it, tiny little accordion folds. "Wish I could smoke in here."

"You want to go outside?"

"No. Don't have any on me. I quit three years ago. Doesn't mean I don't want one."

"Anyway, after that I decided to visit again. I wanted to surprise her for her birthday. I called the day before I was going to arrive. She got very strange, very nervous. Told me she'd call me back, that she thought they might have plans but she didn't want to disappoint me. Plans? It was the middle of the school season. She called me back and said it was fine. The plans they'd had to visit some park could be rescheduled."

"I felt bad. I didn't know the school schedule. Maybe it was some special holiday. I decided they did have plans and I was being an obnoxious drop in. I bought the best bottle of bourbon I could find. I knew he liked bourbon and it was a sort of apology. You see, I talked myself into thinking it was all in my head again."

"I rented a car and drove to her house. When I got there she was fine, a little talkative for her. It was a Saturday but she said Chuck was working. I asked her to go shopping with me. It was her birthday after all, and I'd planned to buy her something there rather than try to pack something on the plane. Besides, we didn't have the same taste in anything. She didn't want to go but I insisted.

"We went to a clothing store in Anchorage and tried on all kinds of crazy stuff. Super sexy dresses, fur covered hats, coats that looked like we were wearing a pile of tires. We were acting like kids, laughing, making fun of each other. At some point I walked into her changing room wanting to hand her some crazy thing or other. I surprised her. She had her back to me and was wearing nothing but her underwear."

Jess stopped and picked up her coffee cup, stared into it and said, "Fuck coffee. I wish I had that bourbon." She continued to stare into the cup as she said in the same matter-of-fact tone. "She was covered in bruises. And when I say covered, I mean literally covered, from shoulders to ankles. There were welts too. Thin slashes like a willow switch would leave.

"I lost it. I told her to get dressed. That we were going to the police right then and there. I was so mad I actually saw red. She told me to calm down, that she could explain. We went for a walk in a nearby park. She wouldn't look at me, said she was too embarrassed. Her face was bright red but then it was cold as hell so mine probably was too. She told me they were experimenting with some kinky stuff, bondage and other things. She looked so mortified. Hell—I was mortified—I didn't ask any questions. It was weird though. I didn't see Bev being that kinky, I mean, I'm not exactly vanilla, but Bev?"

She made a dismissive sound and Don forced himself not to smile. It was odd to hear a woman old enough to be his mother, maybe grandmother, talk about vanilla or kink. He realized he hadn't done a good job of hiding his expression when she leaned in, gave him a salacious wink and said, "That's right, I'm not a newbie. I've been married three times, hell I even had a threesome once or maybe twice. The 70's are a little cloudy." She laughed and Don couldn't help laughing with her.

"When we returned, Chuck was back from work. He'd brought her this insane bouquet of roses and lilies that he'd had flown in. There was also this jacket, an amazing leather jacket with native designs I was honestly envious of. She was ecstatic."

"I'm so ashamed. You see, I let it go. I let the idea of embarrassing my sister get in the way of listening to my gut, believing my instincts. I knew what a honeymoon period is. I knew how abusers buy their victims gifts and pretend to be sorry. That it will never happen again. But I just let it go." She knotted her hands into a single fist, tapped her chin.

"The next thing I heard, she was dead. Pneumonia brought on by the complications of surgery to repair a torn spleen. The doctors told me the injury was probably caused by a blunt trauma injury to the abdomen. They didn't say it in so many words, but they meant he'd punched her in the stomach hard enough to cause internal injuries. That's not kinky. That's cruelty. That's abuse. I should have dragged her out of there, made her come home with me."

The waitress came back, removed their plates and

refilled their cups. After she'd gone Jess said, "I hired one of the private investigators my office used now and then. This is what he found. She opened the file on the table. All the proof is in here. Arrests for fights. Where he served. The women who disappeared while he was there."

"What?"

"I know. You'll probably have to read this and then think about it awhile. It took me some time to wrap my brain around it. Mr. Lewis isn't just an abusive asshole who was married to my sister. I'm positive he's a serial killer who killed her and has killed many women. I believe he will keep on killing. We have to stop him."

She put her hand on top of his. It was trembling.

"We will," promised Don.

CHAPTER TWENTY

Thursday, July 21, Morning

Kayla stood unmoving as the vans headlights swept across the hillside, ghosting through the shadows until the van had roared by. If she had stayed on or near the road he'd have seen her. Getting up the hill and into the trees had been the right thing to do, but she still had a way to go.

As soon as the van was out of sight, she sprang to her feet and ran the rest of the way to the top of the hill. The risk of a fall was worth it. She had to know where he was, what he was doing. When she reached the crest, she hunched down and tried to stay hidden while being able to see.

Peering between tangled branches that swept nearly to the ground, she saw that the road wound along the base of the hill she stood on and then curved again, making a long lazy S, before disappearing into the trees. A trail of red dust lingered above the road, marking where the van had traveled. Maybe he'd keep going, wouldn't come back. It was almost too much to hope for. For a moment, she considered moving back down the hill and heading for the highway, but caution told her not yet, not until she was sure he was gone.

Below her a small valley lay deep in shadow, as the sun had yet to reach it. Beyond it stood another hill and beyond it, another. The land here was hills and valleys covered in pine and fir, dry ravines waiting for rain and wide stretches of jagged volcanic rock, like black scars, that would be very hard to cross.

Between the logging road and the highway lay the forest of creaking trees. The lower branches had been removed and the bare trunks and lack of undergrowth gave little cover. She'd be very exposed once she reached them. Maybe she could devise some sort of trap, get a tree to fall when she needed it to. Sure, if she wasn't running . . . if she could take her time . . . if she could think.

Her planning was interrupted by the rumble of the

van returning. It sped to the base of the hill and came to a shuddering stop, dust spewing. It sat for a moment and then the driver backed it into a clear space between trees and shut off the engine. It was so quiet Kayla could hear the engine ticking as it cooled. It was so close she could smell hot rubber and exhaust. She could even see a corner of the white roof, the rest hidden behind branches and the curve of the hillside.

"Come out, come out, wherever you are. Come out, girlie. I know where you are and I know where your boyfriend is and I know where his daddy is too. Should I go see his daddy first or just head straight to the ranch?"

She dropped lower. It was as if he knew exactly where she was. Logic told her that wasn't true. That he was playing the odds and she could be anywhere. His threats were meant to get her to show herself. Her heart hammered and she wanted to run, but forced herself to stay where she was.

She could hear him below, crashing through brush, and realized he was walking into the valley. She crawled forward until she could peer through a parting in the branches. The rising sun made his light-colored shirt almost glow against the darker background. He looked left and right but didn't look up, lending credence to her belief that he didn't know where she was.

Even though she knew he couldn't see her, she had an urge to hold her breath. He moved into the dark valley, scanning the ground, looking for signs of her. He'd find nothing as she hadn't yet reached the valley, but that in itself would be a clue. Maybe, before he realized she hadn't made it that far, she should head back the way she'd come. If he stayed in the valley searching long enough she could probably get to the highway and be gone before he noticed.

There were two problems. She was reluctant to give up the high ground, and once she hit the logging road the red pumice would crunch underfoot, so even if he didn't see her he'd be sure to hear her, and he had the van.

At the far end of the valley, where the land fell and a deep ravine etched a ragged shadow, he'd stopped at the edge and was looking down at something she couldn't see. She was disappointed he'd stopped. Seeing him go over a cliff would have been a huge relief. Instead he turned and was moving away from her toward the next hill. It looked like he planned to climb it and look for her there. He'd overestimated how far she'd gone.

Elated, Kayla decided having the high ground wasn't all that great, and even if he did hear her he'd need time to climb back down the hill, cross the valley and start the van. She could beat him. Well, she was fairly sure she could.

She took a quick look around to orient herself. With the sound of the highway traffic to guide her it wasn't necessary, but she did it from habit. The sun came up in the east. A towering dead tree, with what looked like an untidy eagle's nest in its branches, stood near the top of the hill the man was climbing. That marked north. Beyond the dark slash that was the ravine she could see the top of a red cinder cone glowing in the sun. That was west. If she headed east, keeping the tree to her left and the cone to her right she should find the highway easily. It would also give her a general idea of where her pursuer was.

She backed out of the embrace of the branches, then slowly and carefully worked her way over the ridge and to the other side until she was sure she was no longer visible.

She was moving rapidly down the trail--then she was face first on the ground, gasping for breath, her mind scrambling to understand what had happened.

I fell.

Along with this realization came pain. For a moment, she stayed where she was, categorizing her injuries. Her right knee hurt and when she tried to push herself to her feet a sharp pain shot through her right wrist. She held it up, rotated it slowly. It went through the entire range of motion. She didn't think it was broken and the pain wasn't bad. She used her good hand to help push herself to her feet.

"There she is!"

The shout was so clear it was as if he stood beside her. He'd played her. He'd guessed where she was, maybe caught a glimpse of her on the ridge. He'd pretended he planned to climb the other hill, gave her time to head down and then ran back, probably staying off the road so she didn't hear him coming. He'd circled the hill and was now either at the base of the rock wall or climbing toward her. She didn't bother to learn which. She didn't bother to think at all.

Run!

Back up the trail, over the ridge, past the big tree, slipping and sliding then turning sideways so that it was her good foot that hit the ground first as she flung herself down the other side.

She saw another deer trail, leapt a low growing shrub, managed to skip over several fallen logs without falling and then she was at the base of the next hill, amazed she was still on her feet. There was a twinge in her side, a small cramp. Her breathing was bad, shallow, frightened.

"Breathe deep. Push your diaphragm down." That's what John Bright Feather would tell her to do. John, who had been the head instructor at her last two NMR trainings, was a legend in search and rescue. A retired FBI agent who had once run the Portland Swat Team, he now taught survival training and volunteered with search and rescue.

Stories about his work with the FBI were told and retold. Most retold was the one about the time he tracked two fugitives through Willamette National Park. Exchanging gun fire whenever he got too close, John ran out of ammunition long before they did. Despite this, he continued to track and beleaguer them as much as he could.

He hid underwater naked, surfacing long enough to

tear away one of their packs, and then swam to safety as they fired into the water. When they stopped to rest, or eat, he rolled boulders or logs into their camp.

Eventually they ran out of food and bullets and gave themselves up, asking only that he get them the hell out of there and to a nice warm prison cell.

They had lasted a week with warm coats, boots and provisions. So did John with no coat, wearing a business suit, carrying a pocket knife, but no food.

"No food," he'd scoffed, when she asked him about it. "There's food everywhere, if you know where to look. No need for a fire. Plenty of cover, and besides, if you don't get wet and you don't stop moving, you don't get that cold. I got lucky with the weather and I never stopped moving."

Never stop moving. That's what she had to do. Keep moving. Chuck Lewis might look fit and he might move fast, but he was old and age mattered. It had to matter. It was about the only thing she had on her side.

She considered heading toward the logging road but if he made it to the van he'd run her down in no time. Best to go where the van couldn't. The ravine would be ideal, but it was part of a wide field of volcanic rock that would cut her to bits if she fell. No, her only chance was to get up the next hill, and then the next, moving deeper into the forest. She was younger than he was. Surely, she had more stamina. If she kept moving, kept a steady pace she would wear him down. He's old. Keep moving. The words became a cadence.

She heard the rumble of falling rocks and turned long enough to see him slide the last few feet to the base of the hill, his arms windmilling. He found his balance and started across the valley. He was close. She could hear the crunch, crunch, crunch of dry pinecones, like the sound of tiny breaking bones under his boots.

As she started up the hill the sun rose above the crest, and by the time she reached the half-way mark waves of mist wove round her feet, as the sun baked what little moisture there was out of the soil. Sweat ran down her face and she wiped it away with the back of her hand. He was starting to climb now. She tried not to watch. It slowed her down, messed with her balance.

John Bright Feather had taught a class on fox walking and distance walking. Fox walking was a method some Native Americans used when walking in the woods so they could move quietly without scaring off prey.

Distance walking was how they covered great distances at a steady pace without stopping. Being able to attend his course had been a bright spot in her recovery. It was first time she'd been so focused on something else that she'd been able to forgot about the accident.

"We must be like bears," he'd said, unconsciously touching the bear paw tattoo on his neck. A tattoo he'd confessed to getting as a teen to show what a bad ass he was, and then kept out of respect for what he considered his spirit animal, the black bear.

"Like us, bears can be lazy and loud, stomping around snapping twigs or brushing against things. But when they're hunting they can move quietly. They can move like a shadow through the woods. Ancient people learned from the bear. They learned to step first on the ball of their foot, then roll slowly forward on the side of their foot. If they encountered a limb or anything that might make noise they would simply move their foot to a different spot.

"If you do not feel comfortable stepping first with your heel you may prefer the Cherokee way. Cherokee Indians do the same maneuver only they step first with their toes, and then roll back along the side of their foot."

Kayla found she liked the heel first method. But what good was walking silently going to do for her now? She should have asked John how to make a weapon using a rock and a pinecone.

The hill was getting steeper, but foot rests and hand holds were easier to come by, once she found and began following a gulley washed free of brush by years of water runoff. Brush growing at the edges offered occasional handholds, while the embedded boulders formed a sort of staircase. Careful of rattlesnakes, she warily dug her fingers into cracks in the rocks. The biggest problem was her prosthetic foot. Since she could not feel the ground with it she had to constantly look down to see that it was in a stable spot. She was also worried that the hinge at her ankle would give at the wrong moment. Instead of trusting it she tended to let her left leg hang while she held her weight on her finger tips and used her right foot and leg to hop from place to place.

When she reached the top she looked down. He was even closer. She allowed herself to pause long enough for one deep, sobbing breath and kept going. There was another small valley, no more than a dip and then another steep, tree covered, hill. *Never stop*, she reminded herself.

Time for distance walking. Step forward on your left leg, rock back slightly, rest. Step forward with your right leg, rock back slightly, rest. Repeat. Left leg. Rest. Right leg. Rest. "Am I doing this right?" she asked the sadly absent Bright Feather. Only the nervous chittering of a squirrel answered.

Nearing the top of the second hill she found a field of scree at the base of a crumbling dirt wall embedded with rocks and enough brush to have slowed erosion. She had no idea where her pursuer was. The trees had blocked him from sight for some time. Without her phone she had no way to tell the exact time, but the sun said they'd been out there at least an hour. She could either try to move around the cliff or climb it. Before she'd fully examined the idea of going around she began to climb. Twice her prosthetic foot slid from the narrow ledge she'd placed it on. The lack of sensation was maddening.

Finally, she reached the boulder rimmed ridge and could pull herself over. She found herself in a shallow bowl of wind-swept rock covered with a thin layer of forest debris. She settled flat onto the bumpy surface which gave her the sensation of resting on a giant molar.

Maybe she was getting delirious. Could you get drunk on adrenalin?

Around her she spotted several fist-sized rocks, wind-broken branches and pinecones, all half buried by old pine needles. Maybe she could use one of the branches as a spear of a club. She picked one up, only to have it crumble in her hand, leaving her with a fistful of sawdust. Tossing the remains of the branch away she wiped her hands on her jeans. Some of the sawdust stuck to the sweat trapped under her bracelet and she rubbed it away.

She should get moving. How much time did she have? Cautiously she raised herself up until she could look over the short wall. He was almost directly below, coming out of the tree line about a fourth of the way up, using the same path she'd followed. She'd made up some ground but not much. What had she been thinking? How often had the doctor told her that an amputee like her had to work twenty-five percent harder than a normal person. His age was not as big a handicap. She should have realized that and come up with a better plan. Frustration and helplessness brought a wash of tears. Her knee and wrist still ached from her earlier fall. Her socket liner felt wet and sweat burned in what must be a raw spot. She wanted to rest. Take off the prosthetic and let the cool air dry and sooth it.

"Hey girlie, you ready for some fun?"

He'd stopped half way up, hands on hips, panting a bit. He was just as tired as she was. Maybe more so. She saw that he'd tied something around his arm where she'd stabbed him, maybe a strip of cloth from the hem of his shirt. It made her happy that she'd hurt him. Gave her confidence she could hurt him again.

Kayla stood up. "Hey, this way you son of a bitch," she screamed. All her frustration and anger echoed across the valley.

He stopped in his tracks, looked up. His mistake. The first rock fell short, rolled past him. The second bounced down the hill and hit his ankle. The third smacked into his chest and he roared something unintelligible and rushed up the hill. She knelt, tore rocks and branches from the ground, ripped her fingernails and threw as hard as she could. He put his arms up to protect his head and kept coming.

She kept up the barrage. Kicking rocks loose, scooping them into her hands and throwing with all her might. He made a noise, not a yell of pain exactly, more like a roar of anger. He was down!

Kayla threw everything she could put her hands on, small rocks, bits of pumice that weighed next to nothing, rotten branches, and then she dropped, crawled to the opposite side of the hollow climbed over the side, slid belly first for a few terrifying yards before she was able to get to her feet.

The back of the hill was tricky, steep and slippery with brush to trip her and loose rocks to roll underfoot, but she lucked into discovering a wide gash in the ground, another dry gully. It zigzagged down the hill following the path of least resistance. Kayla sat down, scooted into the knee-deep gully then started to move as fast as she could. The bed of the gully was less difficult than maneuvering through the brush but held its own dangers. The soft soil and tumbled rocks threatened to trip her. She sidestepped along, letting the slope and gravity help her as she dug the edge of her boot into the loose soil.

The gully grew deeper until she found a place where one side was hip high and the other almost to her shoulder. Being able to duck out of sight gave her confidence. She moved into a sprint and was doing so well, running so fast that she almost missed it. The only warning was the smallest glint of sunlight reflecting from its deadly surface.

She dropped on her side, slid feet first, hands tearing at the ground as she desperately tried to stop. But momentum had her and she was moving fast, too fast. At the final moment, when she was sure this was the last mistake she'd ever make, her good foot slammed into a half-buried boulder. The impact sent a shock through her and twisted her onto her back. She slid a few more inches and came to an abrupt stop.

She stayed where she was for a moment then cautiously looked down the length of her body. Just below her knees, no more than an inch above her shins, was a strand of barbed wire, taut as the day it was strung. Just a bit of fencing left behind from some cattle operation. Perfectly harmless, now.

Sitting up she used her hands to leverage herself up until she could pull her legs free. Placing her booted foot on the wire she pushed. It barely moved. She could feel the tension in it. One end was attached to a fence post stuck in the ground on one side of the gully, the other side disappeared into the grass.

If she hadn't seen it in time . . . hadn't dropped. She shook her head at the possibilities that flashed though her mind, each uglier than the last.

Chuck was hurting. Where she'd cut him stung like hell. Then one of the rocks she'd tossed bounced off his elbow and that hurt like a son of a bitch. That's what she'd called him too, son of a bitch. She'd be sorry for that.

"You'll get her soon."

"Damn right," Chuck stood and rubbed at his elbow. It didn't help, and it wasn't his only pain by a long shot. "You see that?" he asked Bev. Girl's a damn cripple. Didn't figure she'd move so fast. Surprised the hell out of me."

"That's why she got away," said Bev.

Chuck thought he detected a note of sarcasm but he figured he'd let her have her moment. After all, he *had* let the little bitch get away. She'd messed him up too. Kicked him square in the face, and though he didn't think it was broken, his nose hurt like hell, his eyes kept tearing up and his sinuses were running like he had a cold. He wiped his nose on his sleeve. Blood. Great. Just great. On top of that his knee was giving him trouble again. That one he couldn't blame on the girl. He'd earned that one in basic.

The guys he'd trained with, they'd love this, watching him get his ass handed to him by a scrawny girl with a missing foot. Or was it a leg? How far up did that plastic thing go? Be fun to find out. He'd tear the damn thing off and toss it into the ravine. See how fast she runs then. The image put a smile on Chuck's face, lit up his blue eyes so they sparkled.

"Are you about ready to get going?" Bev asked.

"Oh, hell yeah."

He rushed up the hill, making for a particular tree. When he reached it he stopped to rest while he picked another goal and then he went for it. In this way he ran, rested and ran until he reached the top. When he saw her he was surprised by how near she was. He rubbed unconsciously at his elbow as he gasped for breath. The last dash had covered the steepest bit of trail and he was worn out.

"She's so close."

"Yeah, I see that," Chuck said. She was sitting on the wall of a fracture that followed the contour of the ravine. She was partly stooped, her arms crossed in front of her stomach. Cramps from running maybe. Out of breath. She looked up, spotted him and jumped from the wall. Her leg seemed to give out and she almost fell but then she recovered and with her arms still pressed against her stomach, she ran.

This was his moment and he knew it. He felt like he figured a bloodhound must when it got scent of blood, or maybe it was fear they smelled. The sight of her propelled him into a jog and then, as she disappeared around a curve in the ravine and the ground smoothed out, into a full out run.

Wire!

He dropped like a rock, slid feet forward like a runner heading for home, his boots scrabbling for purchase.

"Shit."

He felt the barbs bite into his thigh and gritted his teeth against the pain to come. But there was none. His slide had stopped in time. Three shallow cuts and a ruined pair of pants were the only price for not paying attention. He'd been lucky. Using his elbows he worked himself up the hill, away from the wire. Once free of it he slid two fingers into the biggest cut his pants. They came away stained with blood and the sweat on his fingers made the cut sting. More blood on her side. More pain. More for her to pay for. A few more inches and the wire would have bit into his thigh, maybe opened him up to his hip. It could have been an ugly wound with the barbs adding to the fun.

Enjoying his luck, he lay there a moment, catching his breath. Damn woman was smart. He should have missed that nasty trap. Would have if she hadn't shown herself. Pretending to be slow, weak, maybe hurt. That was unfair.

"It was," agreed Bev. *"Unfair and mean. Are you okay?"*

"Yes, I'm fine," he told her with a reassuring smile. "Now you go away. I've got to get my shit together."

"Such language," she said, but smiled back before disappearing to wherever it was she went.

This was the most fun he'd had in years, Chuck decided. And it was going to get even better, once he caught that smart bitch. Oh, he was going to have so much fun. Hell, he might even bring her back here. Show her some fun on the wire.

Time to get back on the trail. Getting to his feet he stepped carefully over the wire. The split in the earth she was traveling curved away and disappeared in the distance.

He could see the girl's head and sometimes her shoulders as the ground rose and fell beside her. She hadn't made up much ground but he was getting tired. If he didn't catch up soon he'd have to go for the .45 he always kept in a holster at the small of his back. He didn't like to use a backup. Hated how it ruined a good time, sort of like ruining the meat by picking shot out of a duck, but with this little sweetie he was thinking it might be the only way to go. Maybe if he just shot her in the leg.

"Has to be the right leg," he said out loud, sorry that Bev wasn't there to share the joke.

Rolling his shoulders a couple times to loosen up, he moved out, double time. He quick jogged past the first sharp bend, and found that a fallen tree nearly blocked the path. Her footprints were clear, easy to follow and she was staying on the trail, which narrowed so much his left shoulder brushed the wall.

The snare jerked him off his feet, banged him head first against the rock-strewn ground, and left him dazed and stupid. Instinctively he tried to jerk free, but that drew the cord even tighter around his right ankle. Chuck fought the snare, kicking and snarling, all rational thought gone as he writhed in the dust, the blood from a fresh cut on his scalp running down the side of his head, filling one of his ears.

Eventually control returned and he could study his situation. He hung, not quite upside down as the end of the snare wasn't tied high enough for that. The taste of dust was in his mouth. He spat.

He tried rolling his ankle. It seemed okay despite the thin cord wrapped around it just above his hiking boot. It was pulled so tight his foot was falling asleep. His head hurt, shoulder hurt, back hurt, knee hurt but he was used to that. It was his hurt pride he was struggling with.

"Son of a bitch."

He managed to sit up a bit, resting on his forearms. A smile slowly lifted his lips, rose to his eyes as Bev whispered in his ear.

"By damn, you're right honey," he told her. "I do know where she lives."

CHAPTER TWENTY-ONE

Wednesday, July 21, Afternoon

Don left Jess at her hotel. She'd take a cab to the Sheriff's Office and repeat her story for the detectives. She'd agreed they didn't need to know everything, such as what time her flight had arrived. Her desire for revenge was fierce and if talking to Don first meant he had the chance to take action that maybe his department couldn't, well, that was fine by her.

As for Don, he'd been so busy keeping the truth about him and Lauren concealed he hadn't had time to spend two minutes thinking about her, being scared for her. What did that make him, a cold-hearted coward? Worse?

She deserved more than that. Right now she was out there with what Jess had convinced him was a serial killer, a man her investigator believed had contact with at least seventeen missing women. Some of those women had eventually been found, raped, beaten to death and left in shallow graves. If true, it put him on the scale of a Gary Ridgway or a Ted Bundy.

Don had to find Lauren and save her and to do that he had to find Chuck Lewis.

"Everyone called him Chuck," Jess had told him. "Good old Chuck. Such a friendly name for a man who beat my sister so badly she had to have surgery to remove her spleen. You need to find good old Chuck and you need to deal with him."

That remembered conversation, her anger, and the way it had fed his own had derailed him, taken him from the path of law to some other path he didn't fully recognize.

The driver behind him honked and he started, then realized he'd been sitting at a green light. He accelerated away from the light and realized he had nowhere to go. Maybe left at the next light, head to Coopers Grill, get a beer, maybe something to eat. He hadn't eaten a damn thing at the restaurant. Food might help him think. Maybe he'd better skip the beer. There had to be something they were missing.

His personal cell rang, or rather thrummed. He pulled it from his pocket and thumbed it and the speaker on.

"Giggler," he answered.

"Don, it's Kayla. Have you seen Stenn?"

"No, sure haven't."

"Are you free?"

"Well, yeah, I mean I'm not working today and Barb's not back in town until this afternoon. What's up?"

"I'm at the Sheriff's Office, in the main lobby on the first floor. The man who took Julie and Lauren, he took me too. He—I—I got away. Can you come get me? I'll tell you the rest then. I'll be inside. I—I don't want to leave the building. I need to see my doctor but I don't want them to give me a ride. How soon can you be here?"

"I'm ten minutes out. Hang tight." He hung up, tossed the phone on the passenger seat, did a quick tire-squealing u-turn and headed downtown.

Stenn sat beside the bed and reached through the rails to hold his father's hand. *Fader*, he corrected himself. He'd always planned to learn Norwegian but the one time they'd traveled there, before his mom died, he'd realized almost everyone in Norway spoke English. Still, it would have been nice to be able to talk to his dad and his cronies in their first language.

Stenn let his thoughts tumble. There was Kayla, so tough, yet kind and funny. She could be the one. Maybe he should ask Fader about the ring his grandmother, or *farmor* since she was his dad's mom, had left for him. Was he ready for that sort of commitment? Was she?

The hay was looking good. First cutting had gone well and though he made sure he was there helping, he could have stayed in bed. His dad's crew and the couple guys they hired from a neighboring ranch knew what they were doing. And though he'd never tell Stenn, the senior Lehrer's days of being able to do heavy physical labor had been over for a while. Stenn had recently realized how much the crew had stepped up to fill the vacuum. There had to be some way to thank them.

He was worried about Bobby. Never seen him drink before, and the way he went after Don, well damn. Not sure what to think about that.

His father's fingers tightened almost imperceptibly. Don watched him come awake, his eyes blinking rapidly at first and then looking around with a slightly bewildered expression until he got his bearings.

"You're in the hospital," he explained. "Nothing bad. Just under observation because you had another small heart attack. It didn't do any damage, but they haven't figured out why."

His father cleared his throat. His hand tightened around Stenn's fingers and in a hoarse whisper he said, "*Det var djevelen ved siden av min seng. De øynene, de forferdelige døde øyne.*"

Stenn could barely make out what he was saying but thought he recognized the Norwegian word for eyes: *Oyne. De oyne.* The eyes. What did it mean? Were his father's eyes bothering him?

Automatically Stenn reached for his phone. He'd installed a translation app a long time ago. Then he remembered where he was. No phones in ICU. There were signs posted everywhere.

"What do you mean?" he asked. "Can you tell me in English?" But his father's medication seemed to be working and he was asleep again.

Bobby Jones poured the last of the booze down the

sink, rinsed the bottle and placed it in the red recycling bin. Julie had taught him about recycling, that it was the right thing to do. More importantly, when he did it she was happy. He liked making her happy. She'd been gone over three weeks, and though he'd decided she was dead—and the ache of that pulsed with each beat of his heart—he didn't know for sure. The uncertainty ate at him. What if she wasn't dead, but lost or trapped somewhere?

At night, in the dark, scenes of her locked in a cage, chained and beaten filled his head like madness. He'd get up and find the bottles he'd bought, drink until he was so drunk he could barely walk, and then pass out in a fever of self-disgust.

Today he'd looked in the mirror and seen his eyes, as red and tortured as those of any drunk he'd ever had to deal with. He looked like someone forgotten, left behind and never sought. The emptiness in his own eyes bothered him so much he had to look away. Where was he? He'd had an identity once. He'd been a small-town boy, a football jock on a very small team, a trainee, a cop, and finally, Julie's guy. He wasn't Julie's guy anymore. She'd never recognize him in this wreck.

With trembling fingers he'd picked up the bottle of shaving cream, sprayed too much into his hand and rubbed it into his sparse beard. Still without looking directly at himself he'd managed to shave. After that he took a shower and got dressed. Now he was cleaning the house. Afterward, given how bad he felt, he figured he'd probably take a nap on the couch.

Pouring out the dregs from the bottles he'd collected around the house was the last thing on the to-do list. Strangely, by then he no longer felt like sleeping. Instead, he was hungry. But there was nothing in the house to eat. He hesitated a moment, then grabbed his car keys.

Barb was mad. Beyond mad. She hit auto dial and again Don's phone went right to voice mail. She didn't bother to leave a message, just hung up.

After a week with her parents, in which she painted her life with Don as such a damn love fest they must think she was either high on something or lying through her teeth, this was the last straw. The last time he'd get away with not answering his phone. It happened too often. She knew something was going on. *He has a girlfriend.* "Shut up," she told the nagging voice. She'd always heard that wives were the first to know and the last to admit. She didn't want to know. She sure as hell wasn't ready to admit.

They were going to make it. There. She'd made up her mind. Now she'd just have to make sure he wanted them to make it too. She looked at her phone but didn't try again. She was too mad to talk to him right now anyway. The kind of talking she wanted to do might require a third party, a damned good counselor. She'd find one, and he'd go if she had to drag him there.

As soon as Stenn walked out the front entrance of the hospital he switched on his phone and took a look at missed calls. Sure enough someone had been trying to reach him. First two calls from Kayla and then four from Don. Don won on numbers and level of curiosity aroused, so he called him first.

"Where have you been?" Don asked in a rush. "Been trying to get you for an hour."

"Up at the hospital. Had the phone off."

"He was at the hospital. Phone was off," Stenn heard him say to someone and then Kayla's voice.

"Oh good. That's a relief."

"Hey, what's going on," Stenn asked, and then, even though he knew the answer, "Was that Kayla?"

"Yes. We need to meet up. We're at the Good Health Clinic on Pine, Dr. Hisikawa's Office. Can you meet Kayla there and when she's done meet me at . . . "

Again, Stenn heard Kayla's voice in the background but couldn't make out what she said.

Then Don said, "Okay. Stenn, after you pick Kayla up, take her home. We'll meet you there."

"Who is we?" asked Stenn.

"Me, Bobby, Jess. I mean, Ms. Locklear, Chuck's sister-in-law. I'll explain more when you get here."

"Wait, why are you at the clinic? Isn't that Kayla's doctor?"

"Yeah she's getting checked out. But don't worry she's fine, just a little banged up. Chuck Lewis grabbed her early this morning, She got free. Don't worry. I'm telling you she's okay." There were mumbled words spoken away from the phone then: "Kayla says to drive carefully, and there's no need for speed. We'll see you soon."

Stenn stood next to his truck with the phone pressed to his ear. Too much information coming too fast. Kayla had been kidnapped? Unlocking the truck, he climbed in backed up, then sped off, chirping his tires.

To hell with driving carefully.

CHAPTER TWENTY-TWO

Thursday, July 10, Afternoon

Stenn found Kayla in the waiting room of her doctor's office, flipping through a magazine. He was shocked at her appearance. Her clothes were torn and dirty. There were scratches on her face and arms; she was shoeless. But it was her eyes that bothered him the most. The way she looked up when the door opened, fear in her eyes, drawing back in her chair until she recognized him.

She smiled then, grabbed the arms of her chair and pushed herself to her feet as he crossed the room. When he reached her she threw her arms around him, a public display of affection that was unlike her. He held her tight, felt her trembling.

"Don said you were kidnapped. What happened? Are

you alright?"

"I'm good. I'm fine," she assured him, stepping back to look up at him but keeping her hands pressed against his hips, her elbows cradled in his hands. She needed to be close. "I spent an hour or so at the LEC telling the detectives what happened, and then had Don drive me here so Dr. H. could check out my leg. It's a little sore from all the running. I'll tell you all about it, but can we get out of here?"

"We can," promised Stenn, then gave her his arm to lean on as he led her to his truck and helped her climb in. As they drove Kayla filled him in about the events of the morning.

"And now," she told him once she was finished, "I need a shower and a drink. Not necessarily in that order."

While Kayla hobbled into the bathroom for her shower, Stenn got busy in the kitchen making sandwiches and heating soup. He was putting together a rum and coke when he heard her call his name. He rushed into the bathroom to find her leaning against the sink, her jeans puddled at her feet and tears streaking down her face.

"What is it?" He asked.

"I can't do it. I can't even get undressed," she sobbed.

The realization of her pain and helplessness tore away any hesitation. With efficient movements, he helped her take off her clothes. When she tried to push him away from the unpleasantness of her damaged leg, he shook his head. Realizing he wasn't going away she reluctantly took off her prosthetic then delicately removed the sock that covered it. He was surprised to see that the stump of her leg was swathed in bandages.

"The doctor tossed my dirty socks and liner and gave me new ones," she told him. She was no longer sobbing but a stray tear slipped down her check. "I'll need a plastic bag to cover it up, to k—k—keep it dry in the shower."

He went to the kitchen and returned with a plastic bread bag and some rubber bands. Kneeling, he slid the plastic over the end of her stump and secured it. He turned on the water, adjusting the temperature, then Kayla let him help her into the shower. She'd had it installed after the accident and the low sill made it easier. She grabbed the safety bar and let go of his arm.

"Okay, I'm good now, thanks," she said, and turned her back to him.

"Oh, no you don't. You don't get rid of me that easily."

"What do you think—?"

Stenn kicked off his boots, then pulled off his t-shirt and dropped his pants and underwear in one seamless motion. He reached down, took off his socks and stepped into the shower, naked yet determined. He knew she was ashamed that he'd seen her leg without the ugly plastic foot, but too bad, she had to get over it if they were ever going to have a real relationship. She started to say something but he'd already decided not to let her get a word in edgewise. Not until he'd had his say.

"I know you don't want me to see you like this," he said with brutal honesty. "I know you think I should keep letting you hide, and I'm not going to say that it didn't take me some time to come to terms with your amputation. It was horrible and of course I felt responsible."

"What?"

"I was your training officer," he explained. "Sometimes I think, if I'd done a better job . . . Then I realize that's just looking for an easy answer. Am I saying you didn't do what you should have? No, you were trained and you did what you had to and a bad thing happened. It wasn't my fault. It wasn't your fault. It just was."

"Also, yes, it's taken me time to be able to look at your injury, I don't know, without cringing, looking away? I admit it. It was hard at first, to see you injured. It took time to get used to, but honestly, not much more than getting used to a bad haircut. I'm not kidding," he said, in answer to the contemptuous twist of her mouth. "It didn't help that you tried to hide it all the time. Familiarity doesn't breed contempt, it breeds acceptance, even comfort. When I look at you I see you. All of you. Just as you are. It's like having a friend with a crooked tooth. Maybe at first the first thing you notice is the tooth, but eventually all you see is the person. Know what I mean?"

Kayla nodded, fresh tears in her eyes. "So it's basically like I have really bad teeth, maybe even a gap?"

"Yes, just like that," Stenn smiled, and was elated when she smiled back. "Now move back and let me in there. You need work, woman. You've got a whole tree stuck in your hair."

Stenn gently removed the slim branch of a juniper, complete with a cluster of tiny pinecones.

As he carefully washed Kayla's hair and then her bruised and battered body, the emotional anguish and stress of being kidnapped and hunted by a madman began to fade, and the logical side of Kayla's personality reasserted itself.

"Remember in the car how I repeated for you the things I told the detectives during my interview?"

"Yes," said Stenn, studiously sliding the sponge down her spine and admiring the way the water beaded—

"I forgot something," she told him, derailing his train of thought. When he was yelling threats at me he mentioned my boyfriend and that helpless old man. I didn't think about it then, but it just occurred to me . . . It could have been your dad he was talking about. Do you think he was threatening to go after your dad?"

"Oh hell. I need my phone. Can you get dressed on your own if I get you to the bedroom?"

"I can do better than that. Hand me a towel and go get my crutches, right side, bedroom closet.

While Stenn paced in the living room, making calls to

hospital security and the sheriff's office, Kayla dried off, dressed, and managed to get into her prosthetic, even though it hurt to do so. She then took her gun out of the lock box in her nightstand and clipped the holster to the front of her black jeans, on the left where it would be easy to reach with her right hand. Her stump ached. No denying that, but the pain pills were kicking in. She had more in her purse and if it got bad she'd take another. The tricky part would be hiding her limp.

As they left the house Kayla was surprised to see her Jeep in the driveway. "I never thought they'd get it towed here so fast. I didn't even hear them arrive."

"We must have been in the shower," said Stenn. "Looks like they fixed the tire too."

"Do you mind if we take it?" Kayla asked. "It's easier for me to get in and out of."

"Sure, no problem."

"I don't know where they left the keys. The mailbox maybe? It doesn't matter. I have a spare." Kayla unlocked the front door, reached in and grabbed the spare set of keys and gave them to Stenn.

As Stenn drove, he told Kayla about the strange conversation he'd had with his father earlier that day.

"He said something about a man standing by his bed, a man with eyes like the devil. I thought he was dreaming, or hallucinating from the drugs."

"He wasn't doing either," said Kayla. "I've seen the man with eyes like the devil. Your father had it right."

CHAPTER TWENTY-THREE

Thursday, July 21, Afternoon

They got to the hospital and learned that Stenn's dad had been moved out of the ICU so they were all able to crowd inside and talk to him. And a crowd it was, with Kayla and Stenn, Bobby, Don and Jess all in attendance. They listened while Kayla told them how angry she figured the Angry Man was when he found the present she'd left him.

"The minute I spotted the van, the idea of him getting free and chasing me down was all I could think of. I had to do something. I'd picked up a sharp rock, a chunk of obsidian earlier, so I used it to cut the tire stems on two of the tires." She laughed, but they didn't join in.

"What else do you remember about the van?" Don asked. "Anything you noticed could help."

"I'll tell you what I told the detectives. It was white. No windows in back. There was a row of those white five-gallon buckets that paint comes in. There was a sign on the side, both sides I think. It said Anderson Painting Company, but they looked and there's no such company listed in the county. Oh, and I gave them the plate number, but when they ran it they found it belonged to a different make and model. He must have switched them out."

"What kind of sign," asked Stenn's father.

Kayla gave him a quizzical look. "What kind?"

"The sign on the van. Was it stuck on? Painted on?"

"Oh," she said, catching on. "Stuck on. It was one of those magnetic things. The kind you can have printed in any print shop."

"You think he brought the sign with him or maybe he got it made here?"

"Dad, do you think—"

"Always a chance. Maybe worth checking," his father suggested.

"How many sign companies are there in this town, ones that make magnetic signs?" Asked Jess eagerly.

"Can't be many," said Stenn. "We need a phone

book."

"Or this crazy new thing called the Internet," suggested Kayla, taking her phone out and opening up a browser.

"There are three," she told them after a moment, "but one seems to only do t-shirts and that sort of thing. The other two are both downtown, not that far apart. One is on Main and the other's on Pine. Should I call them?"

"No, I'd rather talk to them directly," said Stenn. "Don, you and Bobby want to take the one on Main while me and Kayla take the other?"

"Wouldn't it be better to have a police presence with you?" asked Jess. "I know you two were cops but . . . "

"She makes a good point," said Don.

"Okay, so Kayla and I will take Bobby and hit the smaller place on Pine, you and Jess take the one on Main."

"Sounds good," said Don.

"You sure you don't want to stay in the car?" Bobby asked. He'd practically jumped out of the backseat and was standing by as Kayla climbed stiffly from the passenger seat and limped around the car at turtle speed.

"Not on your life," she said, and hurried her pace.

Stenn offered his arm and they followed Bobby into the sign store.

The nondescript building could have been anything. A garage style rolling door and covered parking area gave the impression it had once been a gas station. Inside they, found a square room with windows on two walls, blocked off by a tall reception desk. Two men at computers tucked into piles of paper so high they looked dangerously unstable, were staring into monitors while their fingers stabbed at keyboards. Bobby stopped at the middle of the counter and Kayla and Stenn moved to the right and a little farther back, making him the lead.

Both men were large, sumo wrestler large, with short but thick silver hair receding at the hair line and short beards as white as Santa's. They wore similar wire-framed glasses, and plaid flannel shirts with rolled up sleeves and jeans. The nearest one stood and took the two steps required to reach the counter, rested his forearms on the reception desk, and in a low, rumbly voice said "Peter Lagios. What can I do for you?" He looked at each of them, giving each equal time as his friendly smile reached right up to his eyes.

Kayla immediately liked him, though she couldn't

have explained exactly why.

"We're trying to find a man who might have bought a sign from you," said Bobby. "A magnetic sign." Reaching in his pocket he pulled out his badge and showed it to him then shoved it back in his pocket. "The kind you put on the outside of your door or the side of a van. It said, Anderson Painting Company. Do you remember it?"

"Not off hand. Have to think about it a minute. Anderson Painting Company you say? Boring name. Lacks imagination. Not easy to remember—obviously. Let me ask my brother. Hey, Robert you remember making a sign for the Anderson Paint Company?"

Robert finished typing something and then twisted in his chair. His glasses sat on the very tip of his nose so he was looking over and not through them, but it didn't seem to bother him. He nodded, and looking only at his brother said, "Well sure, but not the Anderson Paint Company, the Anderson Painting Company."

"Yeah, yeah, right. Peter rolled his eyes. The Anderson *Painting* Company."

"It was two months ago. It was done on Monday but he didn't come to get it until Wednesday. It was a quick turnaround."

"You remember all that?" Bobby asked. "

"Well sure," Robert said, still only looking at his brother. "Did not like him. Too fancy. Too spit and polish. Said he would pay extra to get it done in a day or two. Very pushy. Didn't tell him that kind of job is a two day anyway. Paid cash and didn't want to fill out an order form. We always use the order form," he explained carefully. Always. I did not like him."

Kayla realized that Robert was probably somewhere on the autism spectrum. One of those people who are never comfortable with human interaction but may have other skills, such as eidetic memory.

"Is this the guy?" she asked, taking a picture of Chuck Lewis from her pocket. Jess had given Don a stack of them and he'd handed them out to all of them.

Peter carried the picture to his brother who barely glanced at it then said, "Yes, that is the guy. He did not want to fill out the form but he called every day. He called on Tuesday and Wednesday. I told him it was done on Wednesday."

"But I thought you said it was done on Monday?" said his brother.

"I did not like him." Robert said, gave his brother a

sly look, then swung his chair back around to face his monitor.

"Do you remember anything else about him? Did he say anything strange, or do anything else unusual, anything at all?" Bobby pleaded.

"It's okay, Robert. You don't have to work right now. Please answer these people's questions."

Robert dutifully twisted around on his chair and looked up at his brother. Without asking Bobby to repeat himself he said, "I thought it was funny, where he was staying. That was the strange thing."

"Where *was* he staying?" Stenn asked softly, waving the others off before they could ask more.

"You know the red and white place out on the way to the fishing place under the bridge?"

"Crystal Springs?"

"Yeah, where we used to go fishing all the time when we were little. Under the bridge."

"Yes, I remember. Do you mean the old resort?"

"The red and white place."

"Okay, but why do you think the man who ordered the sign lives there?"

"Cause that's where he called from. I recognized the

number right away. Remember that one guy, that guy who wanted us to make a super big sign that said Winding River Resort and Restaurant? That was his number. The same number. He liked his sign. He picked it up on a Friday. He said he almost forgot but he didn't, and he was going to hang it on the weekend, but he said it didn't matter, because he worked just as much on the weekend as he did in the week. I remembered that."

Kayla's heart was pumping so hard she thought it was going to leap from her chest. The rush of blood was a thrumming sound in her ears. She knew the resort they were talking about, but she had to be sure. "Can you tell me how to get there?" she asked as calmly as she could.

"Of course," said Peter. "You drive to the west side of town, you know the nursery out that way?"

"Grace Gardens?" asked Kayla.

"Yes, that's the one. The one with the murders a couple years ago. Remember?"

"Who could forget?" she said. The string of murders that had begun on the grounds of Grace Gardens had filled the news all winter.

"No one," he agreed. "Horrible thing. Anyway, once you get there take Spruce Road and go up the hill. Just on the other side turn left on Witam. You'll see a sign that says Moowat National Forest. Stay on that and when it opens up you'll see a wide spot in the river on your right, that's Crystal Springs. Go over the bridge. After a while the trees will get thick again and you'll see a stand of aspens. Can't miss the white trunks. The resort's right there, on the left side. Two, three-story, red buildings with white trim with the office in between."

Kayla nodded. She'd seen it many times driving out of town to go fishing or boating on the Diamond River and had always wondered who would build a resort in the middle of nothing. There were rarely any cars parked there, and ownership and the name seemed to change annually.

Getting back in the car they called Don to tell him what they'd learned.

"I need to go with you," he insisted. Pick me up at my house. I'll drop Jess off at her hotel and be there in fifteen flat." He hung up without waiting for an answer.

"Shouldn't we call this in?" asked Kayla. There's probably a trooper out there, maybe one of our guys. They could get there faster."

"Or seeing a patrol car could spook him and he'd

disappear," said Bobby.

"We could ask them to go in unmarked?"

"The FBI look like the FBI and they're in the mix now. Besides, how long to set this up. We can be there faster. We know more than they do. You've seen him."

Keyla nodded. There was nothing more to say.

"We're going to pick up Don," Stenn told them.

"Good," said Bobby, surprising Stenn who was sure he'd protest the delay. "Then we can swing by my place on the way back through town."

Stenn caught his eyes in the rear mirror. Shot him a quizzical look.

"Got to pick something up. Won't take long."

Stenn unconsciously mimicked the sign company owner's eye roll. His patience was wearing thin.

As soon as he'd dropped Jess off, Don called Barb to tell her he was coming home but then going right back out. She didn't pick up. Glancing at his watch he realized her plane would have landed about an hour ago. Probably in the shower. He'd offered to take her to the airport and pick her up but she'd told him not to bother, she'd just leave her car in long-term parking. At the time he'd taken it as another sign of how little she needed him. Thinking about it now he realized it was probably her way of being nice and not trying to burden him.

He wasn't sure which was worse, being an ass or being an ass and knowing it. Wouldn't it be great if he could take things back to the beginning? Find some genie's lamp that took him and Barb back to when they were new and everything was right. When did it get so complicated? Why did he have to start seeing Lauren? When the truth about his relationship with Lauren came out Barb would be hurt. But what if it didn't? Should he still tell her, or was that just to make himself feel better. Was there a humble brag in there for him. Hey, yes, I screwed up, but I was honest about it. I want some points for that. Points?

He saw Barb's car in the driveway and pulled in beside it. He'd make a quick dash inside, let her know they were following a lead, and that he wanted to take her out to dinner if he got back in time. He knew just where he'd take her, that dive of a restaurant they used to go to all the time. That was back when he insisted they had to go out on his paycheck. That restaurant was the best he could afford. After they got married money wasn't a problem anymore. Barb insisted on dumping their money into a joint account and though her salary from the gym wasn't much, the monthly check from the trust her grandmother had set up, was a whole lot of much.

Don was surprised to find the front door locked. Then he decided that if Barb was in the shower she might have wanted to feel more secure. He used his key but didn't sense her presence. In the living room the heavy curtains were still drawn. He'd forgotten to open them before leaving that morning, and the room was dim with none of the lamps on. He hit the switch and recessed lights in the ceiling came on.

"Barb?" He jogged across the living room, through the dining room and into the kitchen. He called her name as he looked into the downstairs bath, checked the family room, opened the door to the garage. Nothing there but dust motes and the smell of sawdust and oil from his collection of rarely used woodworking tools.

She must have gone straight up. Practically running, he reached the stairs and took them two at a time, all the while telling himself she must be upstairs, maybe taking a nap. Told himself he'd find her post-shower warm and curled up in bed. Even as the images filled his mind he knew them as lies told to block out the echo of an empty house.

Maybe he could make a deal with the universe, promise when he found her he'd tell her about everything. Not just about Lauren, but the rest of it. The things he'd never shared with her or anyone. He'd let her see him as he really was, a twisted confused kid never worthy of her. He'd beg her forgiveness, do anything, if only she was there. Please, God let her be there.

He smashed his shoulder into the side of the doorway on his way into the bedroom. The empty, unmade bed mocked him. The unorganized pile of magazines and empty water glasses on his side of the bed reminded him what a lazy, thoughtless—no not now, there wasn't time—he had to find her. But even as he looked in the bathroom and then her office and the empty room they'd once christened the nursery he knew she was not in the house.

He hoped it was only that she'd left him. Maybe she'd taken a few things, called a cab and moved into a hotel. For a second he convinced himself. It let him catch his breath, but he couldn't believe the fiction for long.

Why would she leave her car in the driveway?

He clattered down the stairs, ran out to her car. He looked inside, seeing what he'd missed before, her big purse, the one she used for travel, sitting in the passenger well on the floor. He ran back to the house, dug the spare keys out of a drawer in the kitchen, returned to the car. Sweat rolled into his eyes, down his back. He unlocked the trunk. Her rolling bag, the one with the huge purple flowers all over it, lay there like an accusation. She'd wanted a bag she could recognize easily. She'd succeeded. Seeing it was a punch to the gut.

He was standing there, keys clenched between his fingers, hands on the open rim of the trunk when they drove up.

Stenn got out of the car. Saw the look on Don's face.

"She's gone," he said.

He didn't say more but Don understood. He dragged out his phone and called the department, asked to be transferred, and then, "There's been another one. Don Giggler's wife is missing. Can you send someone to his home? Yes, he'll wait for you here. He gave the address and hung up."

Don was shaking his head. "I won't be here. I can't."

"I know. We should hurry. Chuck might not even be at the resort."

"He'll be there," said Don. "I know it."

"Then let's go."

Don climbed into the back seat with Bobby, and Stenn pulled out, chirping the wheels in his hurry.

CHAPTER TWENTY-FOUR

Thursday, July 21, Afternoon

After Chuck worked his way out of the snare Kayla had set for him he'd hurried to his van, only to find it sitting slumped to one side, both tires flat. Smart girl. She hadn't tried to cut the thick tire, instead she'd dug out the stems. He had a spare tire, but only one, so she'd been smart there as well. That was okay, smart could only get you so far. He smiled.

"*What's funny?*" Bev asked.

"Just something I was thinking. Smart can only get her so far, but I know exactly how far because I know where she lives."

After hiking to the highway and catching a ride to the nearest tire store, Chuck hired one of the guys getting off work to drive him back to his car. The young man was even nice enough to help change the two flats, buying the story that he'd been hiking and some kids had messed with his car.

"Everybody thinks they want to be a thug," the kid told him. "Sorry that happened to you." Chuck was so touched he tipped the kid a twenty.

Chuck started to think about Lehrer's girlfriend. No doubt she'd run straight to the cops. Now they were probably all hunkered together trying to figure out who he was, how to catch him. No sense making it easy on them. He'd already stripped the magnetic signs off the van but it was time to ditch it. He was thinking a sedan this time, some no-color color, champagne or beige maybe. An older model, with a big trunk.

For the moment, the van was okay. He'd switched the plates back, stuffed the torn sleeping bag into one of the buckets and tossed it into a dumpster behind the Safeway. He'd put his cap on for that, pulled low over his face so even if he did get picked up on camera—well, who the hell cared about some old man dumping his trash?

Checking his watch, he saw that from the time he'd found the van with two flats to the time he'd made it road ready had taken a smidge over three hours. Not bad, considering, but he still had a lot to do and he could feel it, that sense that told him the tide was changing. He'd always known when it was time to pack it in.

"Nervous, dear?" Beverly asked.

He laughed a little too heartily. "Got a tiny bit of the gollywobbles. But you know, nothing wrong with that."

In fact, his nerves felt jangled, as if short bursts of electricity were shooting through his body, little zaps that were making him jumpy. It didn't help that he needed to replace his supplies nor that he hadn't eaten all day.

"What was it you used to tell me?" Bev asked, *"An ounce of preparation is worth a pound of cure?"*

"Well yeah, that came from Benjamin Franklin but I do believe it."

"Then maybe . . . "

"Dang it woman, I got lucky when I found you. I'm heading right into town and getting what we need."

"Good. I was afraid you were giving up."

"Never. This is for you."

Chuck located a camping goods store in one of the two mini malls. He bought a sage green mummy bag, two bottles of water and a protein bar.

"Gotta keep up the strength," he said to Bev.

"Excuse me, Sir?" said the clerk.

"Uh, nothing. Just talking to myself."

"Yeah, we all do that," the kid lied, a patronizing smirk on his face. Chuck considered how nice it would sound to crack the kid's skull. Knock that smile right off. That was for sure. But he had business to take care of, pleasant business. He took his change—cash was the only way to go—and got the hell out of there.

He'd parked far enough out in the lot that there were no cars nearby. He decided to go ahead and lay out the new bag. When he was done, he found he was happy with the muted color. It blended, like camo, into the floor.

Not wanting to chance going to Kayla's, where the cops had probably already set up surveillance, Chuck drove around munching on the protein bar. It was dry and tasted the way he imagined ground cardboard with a side of sawdust would taste. It took both bottles of water to wash it down. At least the water was cold. After chasing that woman all over hell and gone he was thirsty and a little tired, not to mention sore in a good dozen places.

"You'll hurt worse tomorrow," Bev told him.

"I'll take some ibuprofen in a bit. She got me good." His shoulder, elbow and shin ached, but worst was the friction burn on his ankle where the snare had whipped around it. The thin cord had been tough as cable. After he'd cut himself free, he'd cut it lose from the tree she'd tied it to. Now it was coiled up in his pocket. and he had lots of ideas on how he was going to use it.

When he parked across the street from Giggler's he considered getting out and breaking into the house. It might be fun to be sitting there when the cop or his wife got home. Whichever one it was, he'd tie them up and wait for the other one to show. Yes, he could make that interesting. But he had laid out a plan and made a promise to Bev. He'd take their wives or girlfriends, or in the case of Giggler, both. He'd toss their women in the back of the refrigerator truck until they froze to death.

He'd let the three cops stew on that awhile, then he'd come back and pick them off one at a time. With them of course he'd use the gun.

He sat and dozed, listening more than watching for a car to pull in. An old man lost in an unfamiliar neighborhood and in need of a nap—should anyone question him. But he figured no one would. These kinds of neighborhoods were full of working people, women as much as men in this new world. Worked for him. It meant no one was around, not even kids. Summer break used to mean kids wall to wall. He figured the ones that weren't at the mall were parked in front of a big screen TV. Didn't matter to him. As long as the street was deserted and traffic was maybe one car every fifteen minutes or half hour. Yeah, he was fine.

He'd been snoozing along well when the sound of a car slowing woke him. He looked out and sure enough, it was Giggler's fancy ass car and his wife was driving it. After a quick scan up and down the street, Chuck climbed out of the van and crossed the street with a confident stride. His leg hurt but damned if he'd baby it. He held the sap up inside his shirt sleeve, the small end resting on his right palm ready to drop into his hand.

"Miss. Excuse me, Miss," he said walking up to the driver's side of the car as she got out and stood looking over the open door which partly shielded her.

"Yes?" she asked.

He worked the blackjack into his hand until it freed

his sleeve, then he flipped it end-over-end and swung it backhanded. Like a boxer, her head went back and the blow missed, whistling past her nose but not touching her. She bolted, but her thigh bumped into the car's armrest and slowed her down. His left hand snaked out and caught her hair, jerked her head back. She let herself fall, using her weight to pull him off balance but he was too fast. The blackjack slammed into the side of her head. Seeing stars, she went down hard, hitting her head against the fender of the car before sliding to the ground.

She was too heavy to drag to the van. Chuck had planned to give her just little smack, enough to daze her, and then lead her to the van and the waiting bag. Now he had to adjust his plan. Anxiety clawed through his stomach, icy cold like the bottled water he'd just finished. Adrenaline. It felt good to feel to be alive.

Not wanting to draw attention, he walked calmly to the van, started it up and pulled into the Giggler's driveway, at a diagonal to the car. Now, somewhat shielded, he went about the business of getting her into the van. He slid the van's side door open, then knelt beside her. "Come on. Get up," he said, slapping her face lightly. She moaned. Encouraged, he pulled her into a sitting position. Blood trickled from her nose, across her cheek and into her smooth blond hair. Using what was left of his energy he dragged her to her feet and backed her to the van, pushing her inside through the side door. From there it was just a matter of rolling her onto the bag, patting her down for knives, a new part of the routine, and zipping her in.

She flailed her arms trying to break free, but it was too late. As he climbed into his seat Chuck was humming a happy tune. Half an hour to get back to the truck and then the fun began.

"She's pretty," isn't she?" Bev asked. "Did you expect she'd be so pretty?"

"Not pretty as you," Chuck told her. "But yeah, pretty enough."

CHAPTER TWENTY-FIVE

Thursday, July 21, Evening

They skirted the town, taking two bypasses, Stenn keeping his foot flat on the gas pedal. The last thing they needed was to be pulled over, but he was willing to risk it. In the rearview he caught erratic views of Don's white face, his teeth were dug into his lower lip, his eyes looked wild. Sometimes he'd reach up and squeeze the top of Stenn's chair. It was an unconscious gesture, like squeezing one of those stress balls they handed out at work once a year when HR held its health fair. Don didn't think squeezing a lemon would help, unless it was a real lemon going into a drink.

They pulled into Bobby's driveway. Stenn leaned on the horn. The door slammed open and Bobby jogged to the car. He carried a canvas rifle case that he put in the cargo area behind the back seat before climbing in.

"It's not hunting season," said Stenn.

"You sure about that?"

Stenn didn't answer, just backed Kayla's Jeep out of the driveway and headed west. The road began to climb, and as they swept around a gentle curve the nursery came into view. Grace Gardens was a fenced plot that held greenhouses, fields with rows of bushes and small trees, and a store with a wide gravel parking area.

They drove past and Stenn stepped on the gas. Kayla's stomach dropped as they topped the rise and barreled over it without being able to see what lay on the other side. For a moment it seemed as if they were airborne. Kayla swallowed, her stomach left behind. They were close. She could feel it. They were going to catch him, save Barb. They had to. She thought about the man's hands, how strong they were, how he'd slid his palm along her leg. She shuddered.

"You okay?" Stenn asked.

"Just a chill," she told him. It had hit 85 degrees earlier but the temperature was already dropping. In the high desert, it could go as low as 45. But they both knew that wasn't why she'd shivered.

Stenn drove faster as the road opened up ahead and he could see oncoming traffic. They swept past the turn off to the springs. The wide parking area held several trucks, some with boat trailers attached. The windows glinted in the sun.

The white trunks of the aspens came in sight before the resort buildings, which were tucked a few yards back of the main road. Their bright red sides and white trim, which included cut outs of flowers and hearts, looked out of place. It was as if they'd wandered into Hansel and Gretel's place, expanded and redesigned for lots of company.

Afraid they'd have to go looking for the owner, they were happy to find him seated behind the check-in counter. There he perched on a tall stool, parts of an engine laid out on newspaper in front of him, a toolbox full of wrenches and sockets at his elbow. He was older than Kayla had expected, with a pinched face and red hair fading to gray. A red knit cap was on his head and he wore a gray and white striped work shirt, with the name Sam stitched above the pocket.

"Sam," Stenn asked, with a nod to the stitching.

"That's right," he said with a wide, welcoming smile.

"We don't need a room," Stenn said quickly.

The smile faded.

"But we need your help," said Bobby. "Have you seen this guy around?" He held out one of the photographs Jess had given Don.

Sam took a look and said, "Sure. That's Charlie, Charlie Locklear. He rents a room here."

They glanced at each other. "Isn't that Jess' last name?" asked Kayla.

"Yeah," said Don. Chuck Lewis' wife's maiden name. "Son of a bitch. We found him."

"Is he here?" Bobby asked the owner.

"Don't think so. What's this all about?"

"How do you know he's not here?" Bobby demanded. Don put a restraining hand on his shoulder. Bobby shrugged it off, his attention focused on Sam.

"Well, his van's not here. Always parks it round the side there, he said gesturing toward the end of the building.

"What do you know about him?" asked Stenn. "Do you know where he works, where he hangs out?"

"That's a lot of questions," he said, "Why should I answer them? What do you want with the guy?"

"We're with the Sheriff's Office," said Bobby, taking out his badge. After showing it to Sam he clipped it to his belt where it would stay in sight.

"We're looking for him as a possible suspect in a missing persons' case," said Stenn, hoping to play on the man's sympathy. Anything you can tell us might help."

"I see. Well, I don't know much about him." He took his glasses off, scrubbed them clean with the hem of his shirt. "He showed up a couple months ago, right about the time I was ready to reopen. Asked if I could rent him a room by the month. Didn't want to, but as you can see, the place isn't exactly hopping. I went ahead and rented to him for a month and then anther and now we're into the third.

"What does he do all day?" asked Kayla. "Where does he go?"

"Well, he works most days. Has a house painting company, I guess."

"You guess?" asked Stenn,

"Well, it's kinda funny. I always wondered and now with you here asking all these questions. What painter's van did you ever see without a speck of paint on it? It's as clean as my car on the day I take it through the car wash, except for the red dust."

"It has red dust on it?" Kayla asked.

"Yeah, the tires and up along the back panels, like he's been driving in that red cinder from Klamath County. They use it down there on the roads when it snows. Last couple meetings of the county commissioners they were talking about using it in our county. It's light, porous and better than sand to keep you from sliding when it's bad outside and it doesn't mess up the water and stuff the way salt can. Sounded like a smart idea to me, and with the lodge being so far away from town it might bring me more business if people felt safer when they—"

"So you're saying he must have been driving in Klamath County?" Bobby interrupted.

"Not necessarily," Kayla answered for him. "I know of a place where a lumber company used it on some of their roads. It's not far from where he took me."

They looked at each other, tension and hope ramping up in equal amounts.

"When I was trying to get away I saw a red cinder cone in the distance. The loggers wouldn't have wanted to haul stuff from far away, right? If they were using that for their cinder, then the place he's taking them must be close. I know that area was logged a long time ago, decades, so it's overgrown and some of the roads narrow down to nothing. If I wanted a place to hide that wouldn't be a bad choice. Maybe he has a cabin or a camp of some kind in there. Maybe that's where he's taking them?"

"Taking who?" asked Sam.

"Should we check it out?" asked Don, ignoring him. "Or should we check out his room?"

"Hey, wait a minute. I can't let you into a customer's room without a warrant."

"I think we should call Sergeant O'Neill," said Stenn. "Let him know what's going on. Tell him what we've figured out so far. The more bodies we can get out there searching the better our chances. O'Neill can call in search and rescue."

"You can call him from the car, said Don. Barb might be out there right now. I'm not waiting." He was already heading toward the door.

"None of us are," said Bobby.

No one disagreed, and they left the confused lodge owner behind as they hurried to follow Don.

CHAPTER TWENTY-SIX

Thursday, July 21, Evening

Chuck pulled the van up next to the truck. The thing in his head that warned him it was time to move on was clanging like a bell. As soon as he took care of this one he'd move the truck to a new location, far away from where he'd lost blue eye's girl. No doubt the cops were already putting together a search of the area. But it would take them a few hours; they'd probably not even get rolling until early morning.

He climbed out of the van and dragged open the side door. She was squirming around inside the bag, cussing he thought, or at least making a fuss. He grabbed a handful of the fabric and gave it a good shake. She stopped moving.

Making sure he had the blackjack in hand, he slid the

zipper open. It was always a little like opening a package on Christmas morning. He was looking forward to that first glance of tousled hair, wide eyes. But this one was too quick, struggling up out of the bag, a regular dervish. He brought the club down, catching the top of her shoulder. She tried to move away from him but couldn't get far with the bag snugged around her. Still a little too animated for his taste, he gave her another tap with the club.

She held her bound hands in front of her in defense. He brought the club down again, this time against her forearm. Her shriek of pain went through him, burning through his nerves, heating his blood and yes, giving him an erection. No time for that now. Couldn't risk her getting away. *Fool me once.* But he could put her in the cold for a few hours. Take her out and see how grateful she was.

He grabbed her arm, and though it must have hurt, she didn't make a sound. Too bad he had to move this along. He dragged her toward him. She was lying on her stomach, arms stretched above her head, half in and half out of the sleeping bag. He let her go but held the blackjack against the base of her neck.

"Move and I'll beat your head in. You hear me?"

He waited until he saw her nod, the silky blonde hair sliding so sweet he almost couldn't keep himself from touching it, from smelling the perfume of it.

"*Don't you think you'd better hurry, dear?*" asked Beverly in her gentlest voice.

"Yes, of course," he told her calmly. As he reached across her for one of the five-gallon buckets, the club, dangling from his wrist, thudded against the side. She grabbed the edge of the door and pulled herself out of the van. As soon as she landed, he was on her, straddling her, his knees in the dirt. The perfect crease he'd ironed into his jeans surely ruined.

Jamming the end of the club under her chin he pushed her head up and back. "What the hell is wrong with you woman? You think you can do whatever want? You don't know what I can do with this?" He pushed Barbara's head back even farther. She struggled, flailing at him with her fists, but her strikes were ineffective and weak, the pain in her arm and shoulder slowing her down.

He got up, then reached down and pulled her to her feet. Forcing her ahead of him he shoved her toward the trailer. The lowering sun lit up the side of the truck so that it gleamed.

"Faster," he demanded, and when she faltered he swung the club in a smooth, practiced motion and hit her just above the right ear. She went to her knees but the tight grip on the back of her shirt kept her from falling all the way to the ground.

"Get up," he said. "That was a love tap. You want another? Get the hell up."

Head down, in pain and slightly dazed, Barbara's body refused to obey her commands. The giant tires of a diesel truck were so close to her face she could smell rubber, could see the uneven wear of the tread. Waves of dizziness made her feel nauseous and she knelt where she'd fallen, swaying slightly.

She sensed more than saw the door to the back of the truck swing open above her and a line of shadow swept across her. As the club dug into her back between her shoulder blades and the man's hand almost gently gathered a handful of her hair, she willed herself to fight back. Instead she stood trembling, waves of pain and helplessness blocking out everything she'd ever learned about fighting back.

"Get up," he insisted again, this time in a voice that sounded churlish and immature. She managed to stand, keeping her arms, tied at the wrists, tight against her chest. She took a few steps until she stood with her stomach pressed against the bottom edge of the trailer. The cold cut through the thin cloth of her blouse. The man held her there, his fingers wound in her hair, his body pressed against her. He was tall. Barbara's head barely reached his collarbone, he had to bend slightly to rest his chin against the top of her head. She shuddered at this imitation of a lover's embrace.

Holding her against the back of the trailer, Chuck realized that if he could get her to slip off her jeans and then bend her forward . . .

"That's not why we're here. That's not what this is about," wailed Bev. *"This is about revenge and what they did to me."*

"Damn it woman. They're not a threat to you. I told you this before. I never married one of them did I? You're the only one I ever married."

Confused, Barbara stood still. How crazy was he? Could she talk to him? All those self-defense classes and here she stood, hurt, scared, a perfect victim. A victim. A damn victim.

Rage did what fear could not. Barbara spun on her heel, jammed her elbow into the man's hip, felt him turn and turned with him, his arms loose, barely holding her at all.

Chuck felt her tense but wasn't fast enough to block her. The pain of a sharp elbow driven into bone almost made him let her go, but at the last minute he managed to tighten his grip on her hair. Then he got his left arm wrapped around her throat. He pulled her back against him, ignored her kicking feet and lifted her off her feet so she dangled from his arms like a rag doll.

"Did you kill her?" Bev asked, and Chuck was sure he heard a note of eagerness.

"Not yet. Just choked her out a little. She'll wake up soon. He took his arm away from her throat and pushed her into the truck, her legs hanging over the edge. He pulled off her shoes. Not as good as getting her wet. It would take her longer to die, but it would have to do. He shoved her all the way in, pulled the double doors closed and padlocked the door. Once he was able to relax he realized the struggle with her had awakened the sore places the woman from earlier had put there. As he started working on hooking the van to the back of the truck he realized he was sick of these defiant women. It was time to get a little of his own.

He'd drive her to a better location, one he'd scouted earlier. That would give the blondie about two hours in the box. After that he'd give her another taste of the blackjack. Maybe have a little more fun. The second location wasn't as good. No ravine. No easy burial ground. Didn't matter. He'd just had a great idea. Leave this one in the van. The idea of tossing the blue-eyed cop's girlfriend in with a corpse was sort of amusing. "A corpsesicle honey," he told Bev. "Now that's some funny shit."

He went back to the van to tidy up. Roll up the sleeping bag, put the top back on the plastic bucket he'd never fully opened. Humming, as he worked, his good mood restored. "What say we hook up the van and head out of here, Bev my dear?"

"That sounds like a good idea," said Beverly.

"You know, I thought you might say that."

CHAPTER TWENTY-SEVEN

Thursday, July 21, Night

Unconsciously, Kayla rubbed at her left leg just below the knee. The soreness there she could handle. It was real. Not like the burning pain where her toes should be. That was about to drive her mad. It had started while she talked to the detectives. The stress maybe.

Stenn's hand fumbled across the top of her thigh. She looked up, saw he was concentrating on the road and took his hand. He squeezed her fingers, a firm affirmation as comforting as a hug.

Then he took his hand away and put it back on the wheel. They were traveling seventy-five miles an hour down a highway that curved through the mountains and the sun was going down.

"Slow down," Kayla said a short time later.

Stenn did as she asked, braking gently but still making the car rock back and forth on the downgrade.

Kayla was reading the mile markers. "We're close. There, that's it!"

Stenn let the car roll beyond the mile marker and pulled off onto the shoulder, tracks cut into the grass showing where someone else had done the same thing.

Kayla was out of the car before he had a chance to turn the car off.

"Yes, this is the place. I ran down a deer trail then cut down a logging road farther in."

"Why didn't you just run back down the road, flag someone down?"

"I thought I'd be safer in the woods. He had a car, I didn't. I guess I also thought maybe he'd kill anyone who pulled over. I didn't want anyone to die."

"That was damn brave of you," said Don. "I don't think I'd have done it. I'd probably have never thought about him hurting anyone else."

"You never know what will go through your head in a situation like this," Bobby said. "You do what you do."

"True enough," agreed Don.

"You think he brought the others here?" asked Stenn.

"That's what I was just wondering. He was so matter-of-fact about everything. So . . . rehearsed. Yeah, I think so. But I got free before we got to his usual place. I think we're close though. It's perfect country to get lost in. Nobody logging out here, nobody really riding their toys either, not since the fire danger level went up and you can't have a campfire or ride anything without a muffler. I'd say this is the right area."

"Well, we're on the Eulalona/Klamath border. According to what I was able to find on my phone," offered Don, "there's a big cone close by and then not another until you're farther south, into Klamath County.

"Do you have GPS coordinates for that cone?" asked Kayla.

"No. Don't know how to find it."

"Can I use your phone?"

Kayla's fingers ran over the keys as she typed in the USGS and found the map she needed based on the research Don had done. In minutes she had uploaded longitude and latitude and was able to navigate.

"We have to head a little farther west," she directed. "Let's go."

They dove into the car, and Stenn waited for a sleek

black mustang to charge by before sliding in behind it, pushing it as he raced to the destination.

"Okay, I think you can turn here," Kayla directed, looking up from her phone as Stenn spun the wheel and they dropped off the smooth asphalt onto a bumpy road, fishtailing in the gravel and bouncing over ruts.

As they drove into the woods the road became even more difficult to navigate, with deep ruts where rain and tires of heavy logging trucks had torn away the soil.

Stenn forced the Jeep onto the ridges, straddling the deepest ruts. Just when Kayla thought he might have to turn around, the road smoothed out, largely due to the layer of red cinder that had been spread on it. Stenn was able to drive faster, and as the dust rose to cover the sides of the Jeep Kayla said, "This is how his van looked."

"I know, said Stenn. Only how many miles of this is there? And what if he crossed into Klamath County? How many miles of red cinder road do they have?"

Kayla agreed but hated his logic. "Maybe we should go back to where we parked before. Take that road in. Maybe I'm wrong about everything and he would have turned up there even if I hadn't gotten free."

"But you said there wasn't much red cinder there."

Stenn argued.

"That's true. I don't know what to do."

"None of us do." Stenn said.

The trees around them grew taller and denser as they drove, blocking out the setting sun. *If they didn't find him before dark.* Kayla's mind raced with images of Barb smothering inside a perfumed sleeping bag, waiting for the monster to come. She shivered and rested her hand on Stenn's thigh, needing the comfort of human touch.

"Bridge coming up," he said, and took his foot off the accelerator. They slowed as they approached a narrow bridge just wide enough for one vehicle to pass. The tires made an odd echoing washboard sound as they rolled across the heavy planks and the empty spaces between them. Kayla could look down and see glimpses of sparkling water that rushed past at a furious pace.

"Stop. Stop the car!"

Kayla started as Bobby shouted and his hands clenched the back of her seat. Stenn slammed on the brakes and Bobby was out of the car, running back in the direction they'd come. They watched him slide down the bank until he disappeared. Everyone scrambled out of the car and had reached the top of the bank just as Bobby was climbing back up. "I couldn't reach them," he said, gasping for breath and lunging the final step that took him alongside everyone else. "But I got close enough and I know they're hers. Look."

He pointed toward the trunk of a tree that had fallen in the river. The current flowed around it but the branches acted like a net and in the net were leaves, an empty soda can and a pair of sneakers, their strings knotted together.

"He must have thrown them in the river from the bridge. They got caught in that tree and have been here all this time."

"Slow down," cautioned Don. "We don't know where he actually tossed them in the water. It could have been way upstream. Hell, we don't even know for sure that they're Julies."

"Bullshit," raged Bobby. "Lime green with smiley faces painted on them. Her kids loved them. Who the hell else would wear lime green sneakers?"

Kayla saw that tears were cascading down Bobby's face but he made no effort to hide them or wipe them away. Fear and pain moved across his face as he locked eyes with Don.

"But he could have thrown them in here," said Kayla. "It makes sense. He was driving, opened the door and threw them out. He tried to take my shoes off too. I thought it was a trophy thing, but he wouldn't throw away trophies, would he?"

No one answered at first, then Bobby: "I don't care what he does with their shoes. I want to know what he does with them?"

"And Barbara and Lauren?" said Don in a near whisper. Where the hell are they?"

"We can keep going. Follow the road farther in. Maybe we'll spot something, a cabin, or a trailer or something," offered Stenn.

No one had a better idea, so they climbed back into the car.

A quarter mile of slow going and they topped a small rise. Kayla pointed excitedly, "There's the cone. I think it's the same one I saw before."

Stenn turned down the road toward the cone and as they got closer they could see the gouges where heavy equipment had dug into the side of the hill. The same material had been used to pave a level area all around the cone. Stenn pulled up near it and red dust settled around them. They rolled down their windows. Stenn shut off the engine. They heard the rushing water of the nearby river and the distant hoot of an owl.

"There's nothing here," Bobby finally said. "Nothing at all."

"The search teams will be here soon," said Stenn. "They'll find whatever there is to find."

No one said anything in response, and dread filled the silence.

Sitting there, Kayla stared sightlessly into the distance. Then, a glimmer of light caught her eye. She leaned forward. "What—what is . . . "Is that a car? I think I saw something. Headlights. Damn, I think it's a car," she whispered urgently."

"It could be," said Stenn, and he too kept his voice low.

"It could be him," said Kayla, her hand going to the holster on her belt."

"It could be anyone."

"Or it could be him," she insisted. "Go. Go now!"

Stenn backed out and drove without turning the car's lights back on. It wasn't yet fully dark, and he was able to see enough to keep them on the road.

"If that's him then he's close to where I got away. I thought he would be farther. I was wrong. What if I wasted too much time?"

"We don't know that's him, Stenn repeated. "It could be anyone."

Kayla nodded but said nothing.

They approached the bridge, Stenn hunched over the steering wheel, peering through the dash as he tried to keep them out of the ruts in the narrowing road. The others tried to spot the lights they'd seen before, hidden from them now by the vagaries of the landscape.

"Stop," said Bobby as they crept back across the bridge, the earlier thrumming now absent as their tires rolled across each timber at walking speed.

Stenn braked and looked at Bobby in the rearview mirror.

"If we park here we can work our way around him. If he runs this way, he'll be blocked in. If he runs the other way, we'll be there to stop him."

They all realized Bobby's plan was a good one. "Hold on a minute," Stenn said. He reached up and slid aside the cover to the overhead light and removed the bulb. "Little trick a forest ranger friend taught me," he explained.

"Used to sneak up on poachers at night. Now let me position the car better."

Stenn parked the Jeep at a diagonal so that if pushed it wouldn't simply roll away, but would be forced into the low barrier on either side of the bridge. "Okay, I think we're good to go. Anyone armed? I'm not." To the silence that greeted this he said, "I'm not a cop anymore, remember?"

"Here, said Bobby, giving Stenn his handgun. I've got the rifle."

"Thanks."

Bobby got on his knees, reached into the cargo space, took the rifle out of its case and sat back down with it across his lap.

Stenn said, "We'll get out, leave the doors open, no noise. Then move up using whatever cover we find. We want to get beyond him so if he runs he'll run this way. Remember, this may not be the man we're looking for. This could be some kids out having a good time, or some rancher out looking for missing stock, we don't know. So, don't shoot unless you have to." He directed this remark to everyone, but locked his eyes on Bobby's.

Walking along the bridge they were as silent as

ghosts. Then they reached the road. Kayla cringed at every step across the red cinders. Then she remembered this time she was the hunter not the hunted.

They made it across the road to the tree line. Stenn gestured for them to come close and he whispered instructions. "Let's stay behind the tree line. Be careful."

Don and Bobby faded from view almost immediately. Kayla followed Stenn closely, letting his movements guide her and help her avoid obstacles.

Unable to feel the prosthetic foot touch the ground, she had to concentrate on the sound of each step. This habit, which had become nearly unconscious, required more focus in the rough terrain and almost total darkness under the trees. Peering ahead, listening for the sound of her steps, Kayla was so intent that the sound of an engine starting made her jump.

"What is that?" Don asked.

They turned toward the sound and saw the road suddenly lit up by a pair of powerful headlights. A truck, not a van, loomed out of the darkness, and lumbered down the road toward them.

"Is it him?" asked Bobby.

"I don't know. I . . . Yes!" Kayla shouted. "It's him."

As it drew parallel to where they stood hidden in the trees, she spotted the van being towed behind the truck, its familiar white sides gleaming pink under the red glow of the truck's tail lights.

The truck and van moved on, carefully navigating the narrow road, the truck's roof sometimes scraped by a low hanging branch. It turned toward the bridge and they saw the flare of red as the driver touched the brakes. He'd spotted the Jeep angled across his path.

Kayla wondered if he'd stop and get out of the truck to investigate. That would be the best way to take him. Instead she heard the transmission grind and then the truck was moving, still slowly but with obvious intent.

They ran from the trees and into the road, then stood mesmerized as the truck slammed into the Jeep.

The animal scream of bending, tearing metal was an assault. The truck's tires spun, caught, spun again, throwing gouts of dirt and cinders that pinged against the van, filling the air with the smell of dust.

The impact caused the truck's rear to slide to the left while the van's slid to the right, pivoting from the point where it was hitched to the truck, forming a V and wedging the combination between the bridge's guard rails.

They watched the truck's backup lights come on. It rolled back a few feet, pushing the van harder against the bridge rail and then stalled. They heard it start up again, gears grinding and then leaping forward, then the lesser impact as it hit the Jeep again. But the Jeep held and the truck was wedged in place.

In the silence, they heard a new sound. Frantic pounding.

"That's coming from inside the trailer," said Don."

In accord, they left the safety of the tree line and ran toward the sound.

"Barb!"

In response to Don's shout, a shot rang out, but it was Bobby who fell.

Stenn went to him, dropping low. "Get out of here! Get to the van," he commanded the others.

Don and Kayla sprinted across the road, reached the back of the van. Kayla fired past the left rear of the trailer where she thought the shot had come from, but she fired wide, not daring to hit the trailer.

Don popped up to check the inside of the van. "Clear," he reported, hunching down beside Kayla, who had moved up to peer around the left front fender of the van. Looking through the windows of the van she could see the passenger side of the cab but not the driver's side.

From inside the trailer the pounding became even more frantic.

"Barb, it's me. I'm here!" Don shouted.

The sound stopped. She'd heard him.

"Where's Stenn and Bobby?" Don asked.

"I don't know." Kayla turned to look for them.

"Cover us," Stenn called.

Kayla sent another round past the rear of the trailer, hoping to keep the bastard from firing again. Behind her she heard them crossing the road.

"We're good," Stenn shouted breathlessly.

Kayla dropped back to the rear of the van, saw Stenn helping Bobby to sit, propped against a back wheel. He tore off his shirt and started to wrap it around Bobby's leg.

"I've gotta get to the box," Don said, from his position at the front of the van. "Have to get Barb out. Do you hear that?"

Kayla listened, realized there was a sound, a pulsing hum.

"That's a refrigerated trailer," Don explained. "That's the fan running on auxiliary power. I've got to get her out. Now!"

Kayla nodded, but held up her hand and gestured for him to wait. Holding her gun ready, she stepped over the tow hitch, moved to the back of the trailer and chanced a quick look along the driver's side. The door was open, no one in sight. She suspected Chuck was still in the cab, but they didn't have time to deal with him. Don was right. First priority was freeing Barb. Backing away, she stepped back over the tow hitch, took a quick look along the passenger side of the trailer and moved back behind the van. She looked at Don and said, "Go."

Don sprinted to the back of the trailer, fumbled for the door handle and found a padlock. "I'm here," he said but his voice was no more than a low croak. "I'm here," he repeated more loudly.

Three knocks in response. They sounded weak.

Taking the body of the padlock in one hand, Don pulled hard while bringing up his gun and using the grip to hammer against the side of it. "Come on. Come on," he urged. Bobby was always watching Youtube videos and sharing the latest on getting out of restraints, picking locks and opening padlocks. There was one brand with a flaw that made it almost easy to open them, if you knew the trick. Thanks to Bobby, Don knew the trick, but was it—

The lock sagged open; Don tore it loose, let it fall. Holstering his gun, he reached for the door handle, pulled it up and swung the door open. For a moment, he saw nothing but a dark maw. Then there was movement and he saw the glint of her open eyes, made out the shape of her. She was lying on her side near the door facing him.

"You c-c-came," she said, through chattering teeth.

"Always," he told her. Carefully, he worked his arms under her and lifted her from the truck. She was so cold. He wanted to sink down, wrap her in his arms, feel her warmth return, but he was conscious of the fact that he had no idea where the Angry Man might be. He carried her to the back of the van, where Bobby still sat and Stenn stood, gun in his hand. Don sat beside Bobby, pulled Barb onto his lap. He rubbed her arms, trying to bring warmth back into them.

"I'm o-k-k-kay," she said, her teeth chattering. "I wasn't in th-there long. But I got rolled around in there and I-I'm w-w-worried—"

"What, honey?" Don asked, bending closer. Her voice was a hoarse whisper, probably from yelling for help.

"I'm worried," she repeated, "b-b-because I'm p-p-pregnant."

He heard her that time.

So, had Bobby. He put his palm on the back of her hand. It was like touching a corpse. "Julie. Did you—?"

"I'm sorry," she whispered. She took his hand, squeezed. "He told me he killed them, buried them nearby. I'm s-so, so sorry."

"It's okay," he said. "I already knew." Looking up at Stenn he said, "Go get the fucker."

Stenn nodded. "You take care of her and Bobby. Call for paramedics. Send backup when they arrive."

"We have to go now," said Kayla. "We can't lose him."

"Take this," said Bobby and handed her the rifle.

Kayla took the rifle; handed him her handgun. "Just in case," she said.

"I'll go left, you take right," she said to Stenn.

"Okay," Stenn agreed, "but be careful."

Kayla nodded. They moved to the front of the van. Stenn dropped to his hands and knees, looked under the truck, got back up. He turned to Kayla and shook his head.

Together, they approached the trailer, then split up. "He'll see us in his rearview," Stenn warned.

Kayla held the rifle ready. Flashes of the past appeared unasked: the stairway, the shotgun blast, pain, and a kind of fear that turned her bones to dust and transformed hot blood to ice. Her hands trembled.

Not good.

They focused on the cab of the truck as they moved forward, ready to fire at the first movement, expecting to be fired on at any moment. Keyla couldn't help but glance at the roof of the trailer. Unaware that her subconscious had drawn a parallel between the height of the trailer and the height of the staircase where she'd lost her foot. What if he was up there, waiting to shoot down at them?

They reached the cab at the same time. Kayla peered through the open doorway. Saw nothing. The cab wasn't big. No sleeping area. No concealment. "He's not here, she whispered and looked anxiously upward.

Stenn opened the door and stepped onto the running board. Then he climbed higher, stepping from floor to door hinges, hugging the window frame so he could bounce up long enough to get a look at the top of the trailer. He climbed down looked through the cab and met Kayla's eyes across the space lit up by the overhead and the headlights glare. He shook his head.

"Where is he?" Kayla asked.

"Maybe he got out when it stalled, got to the river bank and headed down river, trying to put as much distance between us as he can."

Kayla was sure he was right. Driving up she'd noticed the heavy brush growing between the road and the river. It offered good concealment and was where she would have headed.

They had to climb across the roof of Kayla's Jeep. The crumpled body of her reliable old friend was just another mark against the Angry Man. Though she knew it was ridiculous—the destruction of her car meant nothing compared to the murder of her friends—it made her even more angry. That extra bit of anger seemed to take up a lot of space in her heart. There was no room for the fear that had filled her since being shot. That fear had no place in this new Kayla. Her hands were steady.

As they escaped the glaring light of the truck's

headlights their eyes quickly adjusted to the dark. The appearance of a full moon helped. Walking on the strip of land between the road and the river, they moved carefully, hunching below the tops of the brush. The familiar shape and smell identified them as gooseberries.

They dashed between open spaces, covering each other, senses alert to any sound or motion. When they didn't see him, Kayla wondered if he'd left the river, moved into the woods, or if they'd been wrong and he'd taken the less likely course, upriver.

A few feet away, at a break in the brush, Stenn knelt, staring at something. "This way."

Kayla's stump hurt. It itched and burned and she was sure the rubbed raw places were bleeding again. The bandaging they'd done at the clinic was making things worse. Her socket wasn't fitting as it should. Every step hurt. Not sure how long she'd last, she knew they had to find him soon.

Stenn had drawn far ahead. She'd spent too much time staring into the tree line, or maybe it was the limp, her body's reluctance to take another painful step that was slowing her down.

"Police! Put your hands up. Show me your hands!"

Pain forgotten, Kayla bolted toward the river and Stenn's voice. She charged through a narrow opening, thorns tore her shirt sleeves and left long scratches. Breaking through to the rocky bank, she stumbled, but regained her balance. She reached the edge of the river, water splashed across the toe of her boots.

She recognized Stenn's silhouette against the sparkle of the river. Beyond him in the middle of the river, standing on a sand bar, another darker silhouette stood. She watched as Chuck raised his arms in a classic stance and took aim.

For a moment, nothing happened. Then Keyla saw him move again as he threw what she guessed was the gun. It arched through the air, moonlight glinting from it, then fell in the river with a splash.

Before she could appreciate their luck that he had a defective weapon, she heard a second, louder splash and realized the second silhouette was gone. He'd dived into the water.

The muddy edge of the river crumbled under her boots. She brought the rifle to her shoulder. *"Where are you, girlie?"*

That voice in her head. How many women had heard

that voice, knowing it was the last they'd hear?

"What are you doing?" Stenn asked. "He's not armed. We'll call O'Neill. They'll pick him up downriver."

Kayla had never fired Bobby's rifle. It didn't matter. She knew she had this. Cheek against the sleek walnut stock, staring one-eyed through the sight, it took a moment to find him. Luckily he struck for the middle of the river, where it was calmer and where his progress was marked by the rhythmic splash of each stroke.

She found the dark shape that was his head. Watched as it moved up and down in the water, receding as the river carried him away faster than he could possibly swim. Kayla gauged the speed and distance and led her target as she'd been taught. She put her finger on the trigger, breathed in, breathed out and fired.

Through the scope, she saw a spray of blood and watched the dark shape slip beneath the churning water. Calm slid through her veins. A sense of peace she hadn't felt in a long time. She lowered the rifle, turned to Stenn and smiled.

It was over.

CHAPTER TWENTY-EIGHT

Sunday, February 2, Afternoon

The waiting room of Overlook Hospital's Maternity Unit was not the perky pastel Kayla had dreaded.

Instead the walls were sage green, and lined with a double row of ceramic tiles in yellows, tans and dark browns that held the handprints of the babies born there. Those colors and the natural fiber on the couches whispered nature, even when you weren't listening.

Ironically, Barbara had not elected natural childbirth but instead had insisted on drugs, "lots of drugs!" Kayla smiled at the memory. Picking up a magazine from a stack of them, she began to idly page through. Then, hearing someone come in she looked up to see Bobby.

"How you doing?" he asked, taking a seat across from her.

"I thought you'd left town."

"Almost. House just closed. Rented a trailer for Friday. Not taking much with me."

Kayla nodded her understanding. Bobby had changed so radically in the past seven months. It was hard to believe this was the slightly chubby, easy-going person she'd known. This more chiseled man, with the gaunt face, tousled white-blond hair and careless shave seemed nice enough, but there was a new hardness about him. An aura that seemed to ask others to keep their distance. She hoped going back home where he'd be near family and old friends would bring some of the old Bobby back, but she feared it was wishful thinking.

"Don and Barb are doing well," said Bobby, but Kayla heard a question in his words.

"They're moving to San Francisco," she told him. "You remember Chuck Lewis' sister-in-law? Turns out she's well connected there, and you know how grateful she was. She got him an interview and he's starting a job as a detective. I think he's on a fast track to somewhere, but then, he always was. Barb seems happy."

She didn't share what Barb had shared. That Don had confessed his affair with Lauren and agreed to family therapy. Even more surprising, he was also seeing his own private therapist. A turnaround for a guy who more than once said that counseling was for the gullible and the weak. She took it as a good sign and thought they'd be okay.

"I heard Stenn got a new job too," Bobby was saying, "Something up north."

"Yes," Kayla told him, her expression carefully neutral. "He was offered a position by the City of Portland. With the mounted patrol of all things. Don told me he's got about a week of training left."

"That's gotta be different. Never would have thought of it, but he always did like horses. Makes sense. Speaking of horses: what's he going to do with the ranch? I didn't go to his dad's funeral. Feel bad about that, but I just couldn't handle any more sadness. You know? I've kind of avoided him ever since. Don's the only one of the old crew I ever see. You'd think I'd be maddest at him, but I'm not. I guess punching him that day helped." His smile was fleeting, but Kayla was happy to see it.

"I understand. Honestly," she reassured him. "Carmen, the woman who's been their housekeeper and cook the last couple of years, turns out she has a husband in Mexico. More of an ex-husband I guess. He was living in Mexico, working on a cattle ranch with their oldest son. Stenn helped the son get a work visa, and he's running the place now."

"Hope that's working out."

Kayla shrugged, "I wouldn't know. That was about the last thing he told me before we broke up for good."

Bobby shifted uncomfortably. "I was sorry to hear about that. You two seemed good together."

Kayla lowered her voice, even though they were the only ones in the room. "It was the IA investigation. When he told them Lewis was standing on the sand bar with the gun in his hand when I shot him. That lie—I think it killed his feelings for me."

"Yeah. It's not right, but I guess I get it. Stenn always was more cop than the rest of us. You know what I mean?"

"I do."

"Well, at least you're back on the job. Maybe you don't bleed blue like Stenn but you were a good cop and always seemed happy working there."

"I did, and I am," Kayla agreed.

They fell into a comfortable silence. Each of them

thinking about the past. The recent federal investigation into Charles (Chuck) Lewis had been extensive and reached to foreign lands. He had been good at covering his trail, but it was estimated that he had killed at least nineteen women, and possibly considerably more. The findings had done nothing to change Kayla's sense of guilt. She had none. Not then, and not the night she'd looked through that scope and pulled the trigger, knowing exactly what she was doing, and exactly why.

Just then Don walked in with a bundle held as carefully as a ticking bomb. The smile on his face was a joy to see, and both Kayla and Bobby sprang to their feet to meet the reason for so much happiness.

"Meet Felicia," Don said proudly, and carefully folded back the thin blanket. Small and pink, the baby blinked enormous blue eyes at them, wrinkled her nose as if she were about to sneeze, then closed her eyes and went to sleep.

"I guess she thinks we're boring," said Kayla. Using her forefinger she touched the impossibly small hand. The tiny fingers curled around hers.

"Felicia means great happiness," Don explained.

Kayla smiled. "I'm betting she lives up to it."

EPILOGUE

He rolled onto his back. The motion brought fresh waves of dizziness and the pounding in his head increased until it filled the world.

After a few minutes the pain began to recede and he became aware of other things. He was cold. It was July and the day had been hot but he was soaked, submerged from the chest down, and the river was pure snow melt. If he didn't drag himself out of its icy grasp he'd die of hypothermia, and wouldn't that be a kick in the ass? The universe had a sense of humor he understood, but didn't always appreciate.

Staying as flat and still as possible he dug his heels into the slick mud and algae and pushed. Inch by inch he worked himself up the gentle slope. There was nothing to stop him. No brush or limbs or trees to get in his way. He had lucked into a wide swath of grass that bent before him as he climbed.

The moon had disappeared behind a gathering of dark clouds. It was dark as pitch. A storm was coming, lightning maybe. He thought he'd heard a rumble of thunder but it was hard to tell above the rumble going on in his aching head.

Damn woman had shot him cold. Shot him like a goddamned fish in a barrel. Couldn't decide how he felt about that.

With a final heave, he left the water. His boots were still on, tied and double knotted. He'd have to get those undone, once his fingers were working right again. At the moment they were numb. Almost too numb to reach up and feel the wound in his head. He'd wait a minute. Breathe. Just lay still and breathe.

"*That's a good idea,*" Bev said from somewhere near.

He was too exhausted to answer but he was sure she would understand.

After a short while he tried to clench and unclench his hands and found that he could. He reached up and placed his fingertips on his forehead then slid them slowly to the source of the pain near his temple, afraid of what he'd find. Based on the pain he figured shards of bone, a horrible injury, a loss of blood that would lead to his death.

He was surprised to find that the wound was nothing. Hardly more than a scratch. A furrow cut the skin above his left temple where the bullet had grazed him in passing. It had bled badly, as all head wounds did, but the cold had helped. Had slowed it down. And once he got his t-shirt off and bandaged it, he'd be fine.

He wasn't ready to sit up just yet. No doubt a mild concussion was the cause of the dizziness and mild nausea. He'd had a concussion in the Navy after smacking his head running an obstacle course. It would pass.

"Are you sure?" Bev asked. This time he thought he heard a note of doubt, even sarcasm.

"Shut up, bitch," he snapped, then winced at the fresh pain that sparked through his head. He knew he wasn't angry at Bev. Not good old obedient Beverly. But that woman. The one that thought she got away. She had a lot to learn.

Lying there, thinking of all the myriad things he planned to teach her, brought strength to his body and fresh resolve to his heart.

The black bear snuffled and snorted. There was something in the air. Something that smelled of blood and salt.

The bear had traveled miles, following the scent of a female. July is the mating time for black bears in Oregon and this one had finally found a mate, only to have her taken away by another, larger male. His flesh torn and his desire thwarted, the bear was hungry, frustrated and in pain.

No one in Oregon has ever been killed by a black bear. They are normally cautious animals, more given to displays of threat, swatting the ground, mounting short charges, clacking teeth, and making huffing or growling noises, than to attacking.

This was not a normal bear. This was an angry bear. It had been standing on its hind legs trying to discover where the tantalizing smell came from. Now it knew. It dropped to all fours and moved silently from the tree line into the clearing.

The thing near the water moved, a sudden erratic twitch, the same move a salmon makes twisting across the grass as it tries to regain the river.

With a sudden rush, as silent as the night, the bear

raced across the clearing. The first bite tore off Chuck's scalp, the second tore out his throat.

In the few moments left to him he thought—though he was probably wrong—that he heard Beverly's laugh.

In spring the heavy rains washed the bones down the gentle slope and into the river. No record of a human being killed by a black bear was ever recorded in Oregon.

Pamela Cowan is a Pacific Northwest author best known for her contemporary crime novels. Cowan is the author of the Storm series which includes *Storm Justice* and *Storm Vengeance*, books which follow probation officer, Storm McKenzie, on her single-minded quest for justice. She is also the author of two stand-alone novels based in fictional Eulalona County, Oregon, *Something in the Dark* and *Cold Kill.*

Learn more about her novels and short fiction at pamelacowan.com

www.ingramcontent.com/pod-product-compliance
Lightning Source LLC
Chambersburg PA
CBHW070638180626
46817CB00006B/2163